SHOULD HAPPENS

A Leadership Parable about moving
from a should life to a good life.

Todd Clark

FIRST EDITION: August 2019
Copyright © 2019 by Todd Clark

All Bible quotes, unless otherwise noted are copyright © 1973, 1978, 1984, 2011 by Biblica, Inc.®. Holy Bible, New International Version®, NIV® Used by permission. All rights reserved worldwide.

Matthew 11 translation copyright © 1993, 2002, 2018 by Eugene H. Peterson, The Message (MSG). All rights reserved worldwide.

Isaiah 55 New Living Translation (NLT) Holy Bible, New Living Translation, copyright © 1996, 2004, 2015 by Tyndale House Foundation. Used by permission of Tyndale House Publishers, Inc., Carol Stream, Illinois 60188. All rights reserved.

Cover Design by Thanou Thammavongsa
Printed in the United States of America
ISBN 978-1-7333654-1-3

Special Thanks

To Dr. John Walker, and Blessing Ranch, who helped me recognize what a should looked like a decade ago.

To my son, Cole, my daughter, Ruby, and her husband, Cole Kedney. To their future children, so they will know.

To my wife, René. This book would not exist without her support and love.

We are better together.

I think I should...

Introduction

This is a human parable.

If you're like most people, you live in the shoulds. You are constantly chained by ideas of how your life *should* be, of what you *should* accomplish, of what you *should* be better at. You may feel anxiety about not meeting your *shoulds* each and every day.

What if you could escape that anxiety?

In this book, we'll follow Tom Should, a person much like me, and perhaps much like you.

He's perplexed on a daily basis by his *shoulds,* the larger-than-life ideals imposed upon him. They make it impossible for him to relax and enjoy the life he has, because he's constantly comparing himself to others and imagining the life he thinks he *should* have.

We'll follow Tom on his journey from a *should* life to a *good* life. From questioning his life and all the ways it doesn't meet his expectations to embracing, enjoying, and treasuring the life he does have each and every day.

Letting go of our *shoulds* is not easy. To many of us, it might feel like accepting the unacceptable, becoming less, giving up on our ideals, or thwarting our ambitions.

For that reason, we might never surrender our *shoulds* until we see the power of doing so in action through stories like Tom's.

Tom's story appears religious on the surface, and in a way, it is. He suffers from the *shoulds* that many religious people experience. The shoulds of trying to live a perfect life.

But the process Tom goes through as he learns to love himself and his life is a process all of us go through, religious or not.

This is a human parable. The *shoulds* are blind to age, ethnicity, income and gender, and they represent a pressure that all people face. This is a process of learning firsthand what is truly important – and seeing what you miss when you live each day saturated by the *shoulds*.

Part I: Meet The Shoulds

Chapter 1

Tom didn't know, as he sat in his office, that the next six weeks would change his life forever.

Outside, the first snow of the year had begun to fall. The town of Green Springs bustled with parents, children, shoppers, and the owners of businesses that lined its busy streets.

Tom's family had watched this city turn from a sleepy little town into a busy city full of startups and big box stores over the course of just ten years.

Once, Tom had been proud of his city's growth and change. But today, he wished things would slow down just a little.

He remembered a time when the six weeks surrounding Thanksgiving and Christmas were his favorite season of the year. A time for family, leisurely coffee meetings, kids' choir concerts, football, and food.

He remembered when he and his son would play video games into the early morning hours. They'd secure opening night tickets to holiday blockbuster movies, with an after-midnight visit to Denny's for a grand slam breakfast.

There was something so special about letting kids stay up past their bedtime while school was out. It was like sharing in a secret.

He remembered how he and April, his wife, would go to coffee and sit near a window where they could see the snow fall. They'd talk effortlessly for hours about future dreams as Christmas music played in the background.

This season was a time of celebration, and there was so much to celebrate.

Yet this year, Tom felt he couldn't enjoy any of it.

The pressure of being the leader of a growing church became more intense with each passing year. As Green Springs grew there were more and more people seeking support and advice, more meetings to go to, more social events where he was expected to make an appearance. And there were more and more people joining his church, many of whom were new to the area and longing for community.

Once, his community had felt like a small family. Their needs had been routine and modest, not so different from when his dad was a small town pastor decades ago.

Now, it felt like he was trying to provide daily leadership for a rapidly growing city – which should have made him happy. But it didn't.

A knock at the door intruded on Tom's mental escape. Tom's long-time assistant, Margaret, poked her head into his office.

"Tom, we need your manuscript by noon," she said, and looked at him expectantly.

"Okay, no problem," Tom replied with an automatic smile.

He felt far from okay. In fact, anxiety was eating away at him. But the last thing Margaret needed was to hear that.

Tom's job was to always be the smiling, confident, certain figure that others could lean on in their times of distress. Sharing his distress with them would damage that, he thought.

Who do leaders lean on? He wondered.

He stared again at the blank document on his computer screen. It should, by this point in the week, be filled with dynamic words, wisdom and truth for the nearly twelve hundred people who would gather in just 48 hours for his three identical weekend services at The Springs Community Church.

But what could he say to them? How could he honestly write them words of comfort and joy when he felt stretched to the breaking point himself?

What was once a privilege had now become a pressure that was nearly too heavy to bear. Tom felt like a grand illusionist in a charade that no one was privy to but himself, and it was exhausting.

He knew he should be done with this week's message and on to next week's message. He knew he should be at home with his wife and son instead of in the office on a Friday afternoon.

In his mind, Tom put himself on trial.

The judge he imagined varied by the day. Sometimes it was himself, judging his own failings. Sometimes it was his father, who had worked long hours himself, sacrificing family life to serve the community. And there were days when it was even his wife, whose opinion mattered more than anyone else's in his life.

Sometimes, Tom even imagined God judging him. Some days he felt guilty for assuming he knew what God thought. Other days, it felt exactly right. He felt he was falling short in his responsibilities, and he didn't know why.

But the prosecutor and the jury were always him. Tom, pointing out Tom's own failings and deciding he was guilty.

Why couldn't he be stronger than this? Why couldn't he be better?

As Tom labored late into Friday afternoon to churn out the weekend message, the trial being conducted in his mind moved predictably from himself to others.

Does Margaret have any idea what it takes to produce a message every week? She should sit in my seat for just one day.

The Toms in his imaginary jury box murmured among themselves as he argued his defense.

And what about the congregation? Do people even realize the burden it has become to bless them? The Bible is filled with so many leadership lessons and teachings, and the people's lives with so many problems. Do they have any idea what it takes to find the right thing to say?

A few of the Toms nodded their heads, agreeing with the defendant. But the judge frowned, a deep and familiar scowl.

Tom sighed and closed the document. Then he pulled his journal out of his desk drawer and wrote:

Do people realize how hard it is to make complex things simple?

"They should," Tom said to himself quietly.

As the afternoon approached evening, the courtroom of Tom's mind lumbered forward. Evidence against him was considered. So was evidence for his defense. And finally, it ended up in the only place it could.

5

Tom began to secretly talk to God.

God, I do this for you. I moved here for you, and now it seems that you have moved away from me. What once seemed so easy and came from overflow now seems so difficult. It seems impossible. Where are you?

You owe me, Tom thought to God.

"I spend so much time with people I don't even really know, for you," Tom whispered to himself. "You owe me time with my family."

"I work so hard to lead people. You owe me practical insights and lessons."

"I try so hard to find meaning in this crazy world. You owe me a meaningful message for Sunday!"

"We had an agreement," Tom said out loud. "I would do my part, but so would you."

"I accepted this calling.

"I sacrificed time with my family.

"I kept up my end of the bargain.

"So should you!" Tom shouted, waving his arms at the ceiling tiles above his head.

Margaret burst into the office, her eyes wide with alarm. "Are you okay, Tom? I heard you shout!"

"Thank you, Margaret." Tom smiled mechanically. "I'm fine. Actually, I'm doing great." He lied.

By dinnertime on Friday evening, Tom had a message constructed. He thought it was mediocre at best, but it was all he could do. And Margaret was right: she needed *something* to begin preparations for Sunday. He decided to throw in the towel and head home for the night.

The 7-minute drive home was the time when Tom would attempt to transform himself from frustrated pastor into fun dad. By now, he was pretty good at it. His son, Thomas, had no idea that his dad was stressed and preoccupied with work during the fun times he spent with the family.

Or at least, that was what Tom hoped.

***

At home, April Should glanced at the clock as she did the dishes in the sunny, airy kitchen of the Should family home.

Working from home meant she might see more of her husband, but she felt like Tom was never here.

What has happened to my Tom? she wondered.

And she remembered what life had been like for them twenty years ago, or even ten. She remembered the life she'd thought would last forever.

Now, her husband seemed like a different person.

And she didn't know what was wrong.

Chapter 2

Tom made a commitment to spend all day each Saturday at home with April and Thomas. It was the least he could do for them, and for himself.

The morning began with their Saturday tradition, "cakes on the counter."

It was something that had started years earlier when Thomas had spent the night with a friend. The boys woke up to the "fun dad" of that house cooking pancakes for the boys. Then, instead of using plates, he put the cakes right on the counter, syrup and all. It was all Thomas could talk about when he came home.

Tom was glad to see his son happy and excited, but instead of feeling thankful, he felt resentful and jealous of that father. Now he had one more thing to measure up to.

Tom knew he should be more creative. He knew he needed to make more special memories with his son. So now, cakes on the counter occurred every Saturday. And sometimes, he was able to enjoy it.

Today, Tom watched as Thomas put the syrup on the cakes. The sugary substance ran across the counter in a thick, dark, sticky river.

Thomas was delighted, but Tom saw this weekly ritual as more of a mess than a moment.

Didn't Thomas realize how hard it was to make the counter clean enough to eat off of every Saturday morning? Didn't he realize how hard it was to clean up the sticky syrup and pancake crumbs afterward?

Tom did it because it made Thomas smile, and he kept his own smile on the whole time. But inside, all he could think about was how many more things he'd have to do. Clean the counter, make the pancakes, clean the counter again, and then -

"Thanks, Dad!" Thomas shouted as he stood up from his chair.

Tom knew the routine – now they'd take off to the park to ride their bikes together. Tom had made this Saturday morning pilgrimage with his son every week for the last twelve months like clockwork, yet he could not remember one moment from the previous week's ride.

Tom feared that his lack of being present was actually creating shallow experiences which was yielding weak memories.

Tom followed his son down the green suburban street from a distance, trying not to think about the weekend message. It seemed like the harder he tried to get away from work, the less success he had. It was like the only thing his mind could consider was the opening paragraphs of the weekend script.

Tom began to lag even further behind than usual so he could speak the opening lines out loud without Thomas noticing.

"How are we doing, friends? It's been a great week, right? I am so excited to be with you today and share this message..."

Tom had heard a pastor he greatly respected three years ago at a conference talk about how you should always memorize your message introduction. That, the pastor had said, would allow you to keep your eyes up, not on your notes, and to connect early and effortlessly with your audience. This small but strategic action would make all the difference in how you were received as a communicator.

So this became Tom's burden.

He would spend untold hours rehearsing the first few minutes of the message in his head. It was on a loop, and as soon as his mind was finished, it would start again. Over and over and over, Tom would silently sift through the opening lines.

At this point in his life, this routine was not for the sake of The Springs congregation. It was because he wanted to be viewed as impressive, gifted, spontaneous and captivating. A leader should be all of those things, Tom thought.

So he did what he knew he should do. Tom spent the day mentally marinating on the message with no power to push pause on the loop.

Tom wished he could be more present with his family. He missed the old days of relaxing and creating special moments that he genuinely enjoyed. He didn't understand why he couldn't feel that enjoyment anymore.

He was with his son at the park, for crying out loud! These were the "good ole days" that he would look back on and cherish after Thomas was grown and moved away.

But he also knew how important it was to memorize his message. As his church grew and the pressures of communicating a creative and compelling message had increased, it seemed that both could no longer coexist.

Tom spent the whole day at home.

But he was never really home.

Chapter 3

Tom woke at 5:30am on Sunday morning. The sun wasn't up yet, and most of Green Springs was fast asleep.

April breathed softly beside him, catching up on her much-needed rest. But rising early gave him three private hours before he needed to be at work and this private time was top priority for Tom.

He headed to Ben's Coffee Shop – one of the few stores on Main Street open at this hour. The local coffee shop on the corner was mostly quiet, just the way he liked it.

There was ample seating at this hour, but Tom never noticed the choices and always sat in the same seat. He tucked himself in the back, back in a skinny corner by a window with his Bible and notes. The smell of coffee and the sound of an occasional latte being frothed were therapeutic. As soon as it relaxed, his mind began rehearsing the opening lines of the message.

Had the message been on a loop all night? he wondered.

"Good morning, Tom," said Ben softly, coming to his table. "We have a new coffee. Would you like to try it? It's from Africa." Ben paused, struggling for words to relate to the pastor. "Doesn't the church do stuff in Africa?"

Ben was not a religious man, but everyone in town knew Tom. Sometimes, that was part of his burden. Everyone treated him with a certain distance, the reverence of a well-known personality. Tom sighed.

"Yes, we have been doing mission work in Africa for nearly three years now," he confirmed. "I'd say about 19 Springers have made the trip to serve. And sure. I'll have some coffee." He didn't bother to explain which countries in Africa they'd been to, or ask which country the new coffee came from. He wanted to be alone.

"So, I guess you are going to work today," Ben continued, as he moved to pour Tom's coffee.

"Yes, indeed." Tom replied. *I work every day,* he thought. Then he suddenly realized: Ben probably thought this was the only day he worked all week. How many other people thought that?

They should realize how hard I work, he thought. What must it be like to think that your pastor only worked one day each week?

Tom sat staring at his notes for another 40 minutes, willing his brain to come up with something fresh and new. He went through a free refill on his coffee, then took off for the church. He had to be in his office and sitting at his desk by 8:50am in order to be on time for the day's three services.

His message was no better than it had been when he started the day, but he begged God to bless it anyway and allow his endlessly rehearsed introduction to go off without a hitch.

When Tom took the stage, the bright lights almost blinded him to the people sitting in the chairs. They watched him with eager, expectant faces, looking forward to hearing a good word.

He successfully delivered identical messages throughout his three daily services with apparent ease, skill and passion. Not a person in the congregation or on his staff was the wiser as to how much he had struggled to create them.

And that, Tom thought, was how it should be. Tom was respected, and expected to make every week count – and he did.

In between each message Tom fought off guilt as he snuck into his office and closed his door. Escaping the lobby full of people was like feeling a weight lifted from his shoulders. And he shouldn't feel that way. He should be eager to serve their every need. That was what his life was about.

As he sat in his chair looking out of his office window, he could see people leaving one service and arriving for the next. More people to lead. More people's burdens to bear.

Tom knew he should be down in the lobby or parking lot greeting people, but he couldn't bring himself to go down there. There would be hundreds of people who wanted to talk about the message and tell him about their kids, or their new car, or their family member's cancer diagnosis.

They would want praise, comfort, and kindness. They would want guidance and strength. They would want him to have the perfect words and wisdom for all of them – all thousand-plus people who packed the church during each of the day's three services.

Green Springs was truly a kaleidoscope of people. Some would always find a way to listen to others, making Tom's job easier. Others craved the pastor's attention, and the attention of anyone around them.

Tom's job was heavy and awesome and hard. Once, it had felt easy and light. He knew he should still want to do it, but lately, it just felt like too much.

Tom knew he should be strong and caring enough to carry people's problems. This is what he had signed up for. He should be listening...

Greeting people.

Encouraging people.

Praying with people.

At least smiling.

But he couldn't smile.

Once, this job had made him so happy. When the family had first moved to Green Springs, he'd been unable to imagine any other life.

But in the years since, something had changed. How did he get here?

***

Sundays always tested Tom. The exhaustion from leading people wore away at him, and his face felt the tightness of putting on a perfect smile all weekend. To make matters worse, he felt guilty for being exhausted by such good and loving people.

When the last service was over Tom retreated to a familiar place to lick his weekend wounds.

His private cabin was only fifty minutes from Green Springs, but when he was there he felt a million miles away. Trees and misty mountain air surrounded the cabin on all sides as far as the eye could see. The only intrusion was the thin ribbon of the highway Tom turned off to take the hidden dirt road to his weekend refuge.

This was a nearby, faraway place. It was a place where he could consider all he should have done this past week, and all he should be doing this coming week.

Once, his time alone here had helped him to relax and recover. It had given him perspective. But now it only seemed to add to the hurt. Instead of losing himself in the beauty of nature, he knew he'd spend the evening thinking about all the things he needed to be doing – and how incapable he felt of doing them.

Tom opened an IPA microbrew beer from Green Springs' local brewery and thought of his dad.

"If he knew that as a pastor, I was drinking a beer..." he muttered to himself.

Tom let the thought go. He knew the condemnation that would result if he followed that familiar path to the end.

★★★

Tom's father had also been named Tom. Tom Should – a good, solid name. Tom was the second Should to bear that name. His son, Thomas, would be the third.

Tom's father had been raised in a family that was religious, but far from God. They went to church occasionally and never missed Christmas or Easter. His grandfather had been a hard man who had judged himself and others harshly. Still, his family worked hard and felt that by working hard and being born in America they were validated with God.

They had created a good life for their son, and Tom had always felt pride in the Should name and family.

Tom's dad had been the first in his family to go to college, earning a degree in business. Opening several small businesses across the decades, their family lived quite well. But always traveling here and there for business kept Tom Should Sr. busy.

Tom Jr. never spent much time with his dad as a child, and when he did he remembered being anxious about whether he was everything his father thought he should be.

His father paid the bills, and Tom's mom was truly unique in her ability to balance so much. She not only cared for the home and family, but she also tutored Tom when he was unsure in his studies, took him to his soccer practices, and even volunteered as a coach. She went as a sponsor to his summer camp. She made him breakfast most mornings and stayed up late to listen to his heart after awkward dates.

Tom felt like his mother also played the role of his father in their family.

One summer, on a rare weekend when Tom Sr. was home, the family was invited by a neighbor to an event at the local minor league baseball stadium.

"There will be great music, great food, and a world renowned evangelist will be speaking. You might have seen him on TV – he's famous." That piqued Tom Jr.'s interest.

"Why don't you come with us?" the neighbor asked, and Tom Jr. looked up at his dad, praying he would agree.

Tom Sr.'s face split into a grin. "Any excuse to go to the stadium," he declared. Tom Sr. loved baseball and nothing made him feel more American than being at the ballpark.

And so, the whole Should family went.

The stadium was filled with a roaring crowd. The famous communicator looked tiny from where Tom sat in the bleachers, but everyone in the stadium seemed focused on him. Young Tom was in awe. His teenage mind meandered through most of the message, often imagining himself on the stage, the center of all that attention.

That's what a man should be like, he thought. Someone that famous was clearly doing something right.

It was near the end of the message that Tom's mom tapped him on the shoulder and brought him back to reality.

"Most people in this world miss God and His one and only son Jesus by about 18 inches," the tiny speaker declared from the stage below, his voice huge as it resonated from the loudspeakers. "They have Him in their head, but He never makes it to their heart. You know the signs of having Jesus in your heart? Love. God is love. If you don't have love in your heart, you don't have Jesus in your heart!"

An interesting picture, Tom thought in his head. He glanced from side to side at his parents, who were watching the man on the stage raptly.

"If you need Jesus in your life today.

"If you need more love in your heart.

"If you want to spend eternity with God in heaven when you die … walk forward today," the evangelist said. Many people in the crowd cheered and waved their arms. Tom felt himself caught up in the swell of their excitement.

If you need more love in your heart.

And then a band began to play, and a guy with long hair started to sing a song that Tom had never heard before.

The song talked about coming to God "Just as I am." It talked about not waiting to be cleansed or perfect, but coming to God despite all your flaws. It talked about being tossed by doubts, fears, and conflict, but being accepted by God anyway.

Before he knew it, Tom Jr. began to cry. Then he looked up, and saw that his dad was crying too.

That evening at the ballpark changed everything.

Chapter 4

Tom's father continued to travel for business three to four days during the week, but made sure he was home every weekend to take his family to church. During his middle school years, Tom watched his father become more and more involved with the small local church.

Church became like baseball. But now his dad was a player, not just a fan.

The church's exterior was mostly white and aging, like the people that came for services every Sunday. Its original faded blue paint was visible in places where the new white paint was peeling off. The church had a lot of colorful stained glass windows and a bell that rang every hour in a tower. The building was eerie and intriguing, and just four blocks from the Should house.

Over time, Tom's dad began serving more and more in the church. He traveled less during the week and spent more time walking down to the church in the afternoons.

Sometimes he would come home from work to eat lunch, and instead of going back to the office in the afternoon, he would walk to the church with a coffee and the Bible he had received that day at the baseball stadium.

Tom liked that his dad was in town, but he still felt far away. Just as his businesses had once consumed all of his time, now it was the church.

Tom, Sr. eventually became an obvious choice for church elder. He officially joined the leadership team the year Tom started high school. He quickly became sought-out and respected as he began lending his business advice to the team of lay leaders and seminary-trained theologians.

With Tom Sr.'s help, the church grew. He taught the elders how to make it more appealing to young people, like his customers. He taught them how to reach new audiences and share their message outside the small church community that already existed.

Soon, it seemed like the church could not operate without Tom

Should Sr. It was a distinguished position, and Tom Should Jr. felt proud of his father's notoriety.

One day after school, Tom Jr. was running around the track doing warm up laps with some friends. They boys slowed to a stop as another student ran up to them, out of breath.

"Hey," he panted when he reached them, "did you hear that the pastor passed away? You know, the one from the church up the street? They say he choked on a pickle!"

The other boys weren't sure whether to frown or laugh at that. "A pickle? What a weird way to go!"

But Tom was thinking something else. His heart raced. He only saw the pastor on Sundays, but his dad spent so much time with the man that he felt like part of the family. If this was true, surely his father would be upset. Surely this was the family's business.

Tom Jr. quickly found an exit in the chain link fence that surrounded the track and ran home, still in his track uniform, to investigate.

The next 72 hours were spent at the church. Tom Sr. stepped into a leadership role as the other elders were shaken by the surprise and confusion of it all.

People were consoled.

Meals were prepared.

Programs were printed.

Stages were cleared.

Flowers were delivered.

Eulogies were written.

Technology was tested.

Families were greeted.

And on a foggy Thursday morning, the pastor's funeral began.

Tom's father played a big part in officiating the funeral. In the last few years, the late pastor had become his close friend and confidant. Everyone in the church trusted him to speak well of the beloved pastor. And his cool head despite the chaotic circumstances helped.

The afternoon of the funeral, Tom and his mother came home

in silence. But Tom's dad was at the church with the elders until long past midnight.

That was when life changed, again.

In the absence of a clear successor to the late pastor, Tom's dad was asked to consider becoming an interim pastor of the small country church.

The elders assured him that he could continue to run his business while also seeing to the affairs of the church. It was only until someone more suitable was found, they promised him. They wouldn't ask him to leave his business and take on a permanent obligation.

Tom Should Sr. talked to his family.

"It seems like a good thing," Tom's mom said, though her knuckles were white as she clasped her hands together tightly. "That church has been so good for you."

Tom Jr. said nothing. The church *had* been good for him, and for his dad. But his dad becoming a pastor certainly wouldn't mean Tom Jr. got to see more of him.

And so, Tom Sr. accepted the interim position, and announced the decision to the congregation that Sunday morning.

Like the Shoulds always had, Tom Sr. jumped in with both feet.

Just as Tom Sr. had worked day in and day out for a decade growing his business, the church now became the family business. Tom Should Sr. spent most of his son's high school career at the church. He was kinder and gentler when Tom saw him than he had been when he just ran the business, and Tom was thankful for that. But he still left early and came home late most days.

Tom knew it was a noble thing his dad was doing. He was helping everyone, not just the Should family. He expressed approval on the outside.

But inside, he felt abandoned. In truth, he felt like he was in competition with God for his father. And he was losing.

At times, Tom felt his father was giving his best to those he knew the least.

He knew he shouldn't feel that way.
But he did.

Chapter 5

Tom Should Jr. grew in his father's image.

Just as his father was widely loved and respected, Tom resolved to be the same way himself. Just as his father had always been the best in their small town at business, Tom Jr. resolved to be the most charismatic and persuasive person in his high school. People loved and respected those who could lead like that.

In his teenage years, radio and television were Tom Jr.'s passion. He would spend hours in his room listening to sports broadcasters practice their craft on his little solid-state silver chrome radio.

These were people who could make you feel anything with their voices. They could craft a whole reality with words.

He could imitate every vocal inflection.

He learned to reproduce passion.

He became very comfortable performing with no one in the room.

Tom would also listen to famous preachers from time to time. Ever since his family's life-changing experience a decade ago, he was inspired by the skills of these famous communicators.

As he made his way through high school, his popularity, confidence, and ability to persuade grew.

On a regular basis Tom would fail to study for a test because he knew he could talk almost any teacher into a passing grade. People seemed to like him if he spoke beautifully to them even more than if he worked hard or did a good job.

He talked himself into dates with the most popular girls in school.

He talked himself into numerous jobs, which he would keep until a better one came along. Then he would wiggle his way into that one, leaving the old one behind.

It seemed like he could talk anyone into just about anything.

Tom loved to imitate his father's business skills, and he was very successful. He could make as much money in one afternoon of buying and selling baseball cards as his high school friends would make in a whole week flipping burgers or mowing lawns.

Tom loved the challenge of making money even more than he loved having money. But when it came to work, he was not sure who he wanted to invest in more: himself, or God.

God had changed his life for the better, bringing his father home and bringing love into his life. But as Tom watched his father, he realized his new role meant not much time for himself and not much money. These were noble choices his father was making, and money surely wasn't everything.

But it's something, Tom thought to himself.

Tom was wise enough to know even as a senior in high school that if he really put his mind to it, he could probably make a lot of money. He could buy a nice car, probably a sports car. He could live near the beach. He could be a person that people admired. If he put his mind to it and worked hard - mainly for himself.

He had also learned from watching his father that pastors didn't drive Porsches. And they didn't live on tropical islands or near the beach unless they were missionaries. They were loved and respected – but only in a certain way. To Tom Jr., the pastor's role seemed limited.

After high school graduation, Tom began his career in communications. He was accepted on a full ride scholarship to a prestigious East Coast Ivy League school, and everyone in town was proud of him.

Tom Should stood out.

And he loved it.

This, Tom thought, *is what I was meant to do.*

✱✱✱

The East Coast college town was very different - but not in all the ways Tom had hoped for or expected.

He'd thought that the people here should be different from the people of his small hometown. More extraordinary.

More hard-working. Like him.

But they weren't. They spoke differently and dressed differently, but they still did the same old things that drove Tom crazy back home. They slacked off. They made mistakes. They wasted time. They accepted less than the best.

After a few weeks, his feelings about the place were less than magical. It didn't live up to the hype of the website and student ambassadors that had courted him. Tom felt that the school was failing its obligations – and failing him.

It was during his freshman year that Tom found out just how often others fell short of his expectations. Far short, actually.

On three occasions, there were group projects in his Intro to Communications class. And each time, Tom had switched groups because his peers seemed to have no work ethic or sense of pride in the finished product. They had shut down as soon as he began to explain his ideas and left him to do all the work himself.

And that wasn't the only time his peers fell short of his expectations.

Tom was amazed at how easygoing and carefree so many other students often seemed, when he felt quite sober and saddled with weighty ideas that he would ride quietly around in his mind. This was the time in life to make something of himself. How could the others be so casual about it?

Eventually, Tom was appalled at them rather than amazed. How could they stand to wile away the time in the dorms and on the grassy green lawns around campus, pranking each other instead of studying? How could they stand to have parties when there were always exam deadlines looming?

The ideas that he rode around in his mind became a safe retreat from those who were wasting time and simply having fun. He told himself he would outdo them all.

Tom spent much of that first year seeking a friend group that lived up to his unrealistic expectations, academically and socially. But Tom found that even students who seemed ambitious at first often spent a lot of time goofing off, doing nothing. Then they'd have the nerve to blame *him* when he tried to get the group back on-target.

Because his would-be friends hardly ever acted like Tom thought they should, it was not a stellar year in the friendship department.

Tom was lonely. But he chalked it up to having lofty goals and healthy ambitions. He couldn't be expected to compromise just to have friends, could he?

When summer came, Tom was eager to get home.

Back home, people like his father understood the value of hard work. Even if they didn't always live up to Tom's extraordinary expectations, either.

Chapter 6

The summer after his freshman year of college, Tom began to feel like he was really getting somewhere. Despite returning to his very ordinary hometown, he had several unique and solid summer job opportunities to choose from.

But having many options raised a new problem. His mind became a torture chamber as he constantly marinated in the possibilities. He had to make the best choice. Which one should he choose?

Should he try to make money this summer and start saving for his future? Then he should accept the construction job.

Should he try to gain work experience in his field of communication? Then he should accept the unpaid internship at the local 80's radio station and become a nighttime DJ.

Should he just have fun?

So many of his high school friends were also back home from college, and none of them seemed worried at all about a job. They seemed to just live in the moment, enjoying their time without looking ahead. Maybe he should just be a lifeguard at the city pool and hang out at the small-town Sonic with everyone each night.

Part of him longed for that carefree life. But he couldn't stop worrying about money and about his career.

Tom's parents said he should make money at every opportunity, as they had done. But Tom Jr. disagreed. Experience in communications would be much more valuable in the long run when he graduated and was qualified for much higher-paying jobs.

And after hundreds of hours of mental gymnastics, Tom accepted the unpaid internship at the local radio station.

When he showed up to the radio station and saw the equipment laid out before him, Tom Should felt good.

And not just good. He felt better than pretty much everyone else, including his parents. He made the choice that would further his career in communications. It was the right choice.

At night, he would captivate everyone who listened to the radio with his voice. And years from now, he would be happier and more successful because of it.

Of course, this meant that Tom would be sleeping during the day to stay awake at night. It meant he'd be missing out on pool parties and summer hang-outs.

But this was definitely what he should do.

Tom's training at the station was short and sweet. The station manager had never been to college and was intimidated by Tom's 28 credit hours from an Ivy League university.

"You'll be fine," the station manager said hastily, and gave Tom his own set of keys for the night shift. Tom looked at those keys and thought about what they represented. Soon, the nighttime airwaves would be his.

On Tom's first night, he lined up the albums to be played. He agonized over what he should play for the few dozen people who would be listening between 11pm and 5am.

REM? REO Speedwagon? Journey? Styxx? 38 Special? Boston?

Finally, Tom made his selection. It was the big 80's, and he was ready to rock.

The first night felt great. Tom was sure he gave all his listeners a great experience, and he felt very confident about his decision to work at the station.

But when Tom arrived at the station on night two the station manager had written him a note that simply said: "Play the playlist!"

What! Play the playlist? I can't even play what I want to play? What was the point of being a late night DJ if he didn't have control over what he played?

Tom was frustrated. In his mind he began to rip apart Roger, the station manager with no formal education.

He should have spoken to me in person.

He should trust me to play good songs.

He should not need to micromanage me.

He should have hired a different intern if all he wants to do is tell people what to do!

"I need to be making money this summer," Tom said aloud to no one. The appeal of this job had been the fame, freedom, and creative control. Now that he knew he was just a lackey, that was gone.

The second night melted into the twentieth night with no distinguishable differences. By the beginning of the third week, Tom's mind was on autopilot each night, and he began to think of what he could do while he was working to redeem this summer.

It was then that Tom realized he should always be doing more than one thing. If he focused on just one pursuit, it would never be enough for him.

And whatever the other thing was for this summer, it needed to make money. In this way, he would get ahead. He never named specific people he was trying to get ahead of. He was trying to get ahead of everyone.

He had spent his life carefully building this construct of what people should be doing, and he applied it to everyone he met.

Whenever he met someone new, he would perform a quiet series of comparisons. Within seconds, he would put a price tag on himself that was either greater than or less than the person in front of him. His goal was to be the most worthy person he knew.

But sometimes, that thought gave him great anxiety. Although he easily outstripped those around him with his talent and hard work, sometimes he wondered: could he reach that goal of ultimate worthiness?

What would happen if he didn't?

Chapter 7

Soon after he realized the job at the radio station would not meet his expectations, Tom found the perfect side hustle. He would sell cars.

Tom could talk anyone into anything – so talking people into going home with a sleek new ride was no problem. The job allowed him to meet people by appointment only and make his own hours, so it fit quite well with his job at the radio station.

Each Monday night Tom would stop by the EZ-GO Gas Station on his way to work and pick up the latest full-color version of the "Wheels & Deals" magazine. He'd have hours throughout the night to read through its glossy pages and learn to identify the best cars and the best prices.

Tom quickly became an expert in identifying sports cars. He could buy used cars from desperate for cash locals, clean them up, and sell them at a generous profit.

Sports cars were in Tom's blood. His dad had owned several sporty cars while Tom was growing up – before he became a pastor.

There was the black and gold 1978 Pontiac Firebird with the shining eagle on the hood.

The 1984 Camaro IROC with white leather seats and a stereo system whose buttons were backlit with bright green lights. The green glow on the white leather interior was the envy of all at a time when such technology was cutting edge.

And finally, there was Tom's favorite car by far. It had been a candy apple red 1982 911 Carrera Porsche. It had all-black wheels, accordion bumpers and black leather interior.

Driving in it, Tom felt like a million bucks. He felt like he belonged to the most successful family in the neighborhood. He felt like he was going places.

Tom dreamed of one day owning that car. He would picture his father throwing him the keys at graduation with the words: "You deserve it, Son."

Surely that would be confirmation that all his hard work and smart decisions had paid off. Then, Tom would drive the car up windy mountain roads or along the Pacific Coast Highway in his mind.

But those dreams evaporated when Tom Should Sr. became the interim pastor of the little church. Suddenly, luxurious cars weren't his dad's priority anymore. Tom Should Sr. said he could think of better uses for that money.

"Pastors don't drive Porsches," his father said and sold the car to a local dentist. He donated the money he made on the sale to a local clinic that offered free healthcare to those in need.

As terrible and unfair as that seemed, Tom also believed it was true. Dentists, not pastors, deserved to drive sporty cars. They had the kind of success that mattered: unhindered success, free from judgment by others.

So, for the last six weeks of summer, Tom played nearly 3,000 songs at the station and sold seven cars. He made over three thousand dollars – a lot of money for a soon-to-be sophomore in college.

Tom Should Jr. was amazingly productive, and his own personal price tag went up dramatically that summer. He felt confident as he stood beside nearly anyone.

He was going places. Most of them weren't.

On August 15th Tom crammed all of his important possessions into his new-to-him, lightly used black with black interior Nissan 300ZX and headed east.

This year of college should be my best yet, he thought, as the auto-reverse tape deck stereo system he had installed sent a green glow on the black leather seats of the car he'd bought for himself. He blasted Boston's *Don't Look Back* on both sides of the tape.

At the rate he was going, Tom knew he'd become the most successful Should yet.

Chapter 8

Tom was prepared to be disappointed when he got back to his East Coast school. He was prepared to find those around him not working hard or not meeting his expectations, as always.

But on the first day of Tom's sophomore year, things changed dramatically.

On the first day of American Literature II, Tom met April.

April was not like any girl Tom had ever met. She had a warm smile, and she never seemed to stop moving. She was like a tornado of activity, and Tom was ready to be blown away with her wherever she wanted to go.

He had been quietly seeking a girl who was gifted and driven, like he was. But most girls had seemed too preoccupied with their studies to have time to get to know him. April was different. She took her studies seriously, and she took life seriously, but she always had time for friends and family.

On the first day of class, April raised her hand and asked the professor what it took to be at the top of his class.

Not what it took to get an A, or a passing grade. What did it require to be the *top* student in the class?

As Tom listened to her ask the question, he realized he was staring. She realized it, too. She met his eyes with a friendly smile, but the smile had a challenge in it.

There could only be one student at the top of the class, and April had already pegged Tom as competition.

Game on, he thought.

April was obviously not satisfied with just getting into an Ivy League school. She had high expectations of herself. She proved that when she beat Tom in their first competition, getting the highest score in the class on the American Lit II midterm.

Tom felt that she might make a great Should someday.

***

April loved so many things about Tom.

She loved him first the way you love a new hobby, or a new song. He was fast-paced. He was exciting. He was driven.

He was everything she wanted to be.

But soon, she found herself wondering: did Tom ever relax?

Did he ever stop and just take time to smell the flowers?

She hoped he would.

***

Soon, Tom found his priorities shifting. Being at the top of the class was no longer the most important thing in his life. Now, April was.

Tom knew that months ago he would have looked down on anyone who spent more time with a girl than he spent studying, but when April was around, that didn't seem to matter.

The first semester flew by as Tom and April attended classes

quickly, so they could slowly spend more time together. Tom no longer obsessed over his studies, and now felt that getting an A

was "good enough" if it meant he got to spend more time with her.

Tom learned a lot about April that semester, and even the odd things felt fantastic. He learned that she hated football, dark chocolate, dogs that shed fur all over everything, and all Nicolas Cage movies.

Tom loved football and chocolate, but none of these were deal breakers in Tom's book. If anything, it was refreshing to meet someone who knew what she liked – and didn't care if others agreed. She didn't change herself for anyone.

But she also respected Tom. He knew that when she bought him an NFL T-shirt and a dark chocolate gift set.

He learned that she loved popcorn with real butter, movies made in the 1980's, live music, soft T-shirts, baby turtles, and skinny margaritas. He scored big points in her book the day he took her to the local nature museum to witness turtles hatching, then out for coffee afterwards.

There was one more thing. April had never been to the ocean. She had never put her toes in the sand.

Tom quietly vowed that one day the two of them would live at the beach with their kids and a dog that didn't shed. He'd try to find a beach with sea turtle nests so that April could volunteer to protect the hatchlings every year as they made their journey to the sea.

Like him, April had grown up in a pastor's home. She came from a little Midwest town that sounded a lot like the movie *Footloose*, with Kevin Bacon, when she described it. It was a life where everyone knows your business and knows how you should act – and April couldn't wait to get out of it.

April didn't always do what she should. She had her own ideas about what was best for her. But what she shouldn't do, she hid quite well when she was back home.

At college she could finally be herself. To Tom, it was like he was watching a flower bloom over the course of a few months.

It was amazing to watch.

April was amazing to watch.

April loved her mom and dad dearly but had decided long ago the life of a pastor's wife would not be the life for her. She said you didn't have to agree with someone to love them. Tom admired her for that.

He also felt relieved. He didn't plan to follow in his father's pastoral footsteps – so he and April were on the same page about their future lives.

That semester held enough memories to fill a decade of life. Tom wished that it could last forever – but he also couldn't wait for the next step.

Whether they were in class, working out in the gym together or listening to music, everything was a competition. Not just between them, but also with everyone around them. They were racing and outpacing people who didn't even know the gun had gone off! Needless to say, they usually won.

Against everyone, except each other.

Tom even argued one afternoon that he was pretty sure he

got more done in his dreams, while he was sleeping, than April did.

April laughed. "Funny," she said, "in my dreams you're always the naked high school freshman who can't remember his locker combination!"

Tom paused. "In your dreams, I'm naked?" he asked.

"Yeah," said April. "But it's not nearly as attractive as you think. In fact, it's often horrifying, and I wake up early just to get away!"

They both laughed. But Tom felt like he won the dream competition, simply by being included in April's subconscious moments. Never mind that he was a naked freshman…she was dreaming about him!

As Christmas break began, it was time for Tom and April to go back to their families. But just before leaving their dorms, Tom approached April with his palms sweating.

Voice shaking, he asked her if she'd want to come spend New Year's Eve at his house. That way, she could meet his mom and dad and more of the Shoulds who would gather for the holiday.

Tom's heart raced in his chest, but it turned out he needn't have worried. April accepted the invitation on the spot.

They kissed and, just like Journey, headed their separate ways living worlds apart.

For now.

Someday, Tom thought, *we should be together.*

★★★

On Thursday, December 30th, April arrived. She surprised Tom a day early.

Tom quickly scraped his calendar clean and spent the uncommonly warm late December day showing April around town.

It was a magical day in the little town. Some people were protesting winter by wearing shorts, already dreaming of Spring. Tom showed April the radio station where he still worked on holidays, but refused to listen to it as they drove around town.

"That station won't even be around a year from now," Tom

explained as he told April about his incarceration at the station the previous summer. "The manager doesn't know what's good, and his listeners know it."

As they drove around, Tom knew everyone they met. Everyone waved, and Tom had a personal story about each of them.

On this day before New Years' Eve, they ended up at the little church where Tom Should Sr. was the pastor.

Tom proudly showed April the new landscaping and paint that his dad had personally completed with his own time and money. He hoped this made a great first impression on April as they entered into the narrow vestibule of the small church.

After an 11-minute tour, April had seen the whole building. The whole of his dad's livelihood. They ended up standing in front of the large, dark wooden door with ornate carvings including what looked like a cross right in the middle.

Next to the door was a black plastic sign with gold letters that said: "Pastor Tom Should."

His heart now pounding again, Tom Jr. knocked. Tom Sr. appeared at the door instantly, as if he'd been supernaturally alerted to their presence.

"Come on in," Tom Sr. said, holding the door open wide.

"Dad," Tom said nervously, "I want you to meet April!"

He wasn't too worried about what his dad thought of April – he'd made up his own mind either way. But he was very nervous about what April would think of his dad! His dad was a businessman turned pastor, where April's dad had been a pastor all his vocational life.

Tom Jr. stood to the side while his dad and April shook hands. April gave his dad the smile Tom knew well. The smile that said she approved.

"It's great to finally meet you, April," Tom Sr. said generously. "Our Tommy has told us so much about you."

"Tommy?" April glanced at Tom, her eyes sparkling. He felt his cheeks burn, but in a good way. She clearly thought the nickname was cute.

"Tell me about your family, April," Tom Sr. requested as he

ushered the two into his office. Tom gave April the plush chair that sat across from his dad's desk and stood against the wall himself.

With that simple invitation, April sprang into a twenty-minute monologue about her parents, siblings, hometown and dreams. She spoke about her father's church, her father and mother's happy marriage, and her little brother who planned to follow in his father's footsteps and become a pastor.

She spoke about her own sleepy little town – much like this one – and her dreams of becoming a mother. Tom noticed that she did not include the part where she hoped to write books one day and wisely excluded the fact that she did not want to be a pastor's wife.

Best of all, she interlaced her whole speech with affection for Tom. She told his father how he was helping her become the person that she dreamed she might one day be. She glanced slyly at him as she spoke – hinting, Tom hoped, that he might someday be the husband she dreamed of.

Finally, April told Tom Sr. that he must meet her dad someday and share pastoral tales. "I'm sure you two would have so much to talk about!"

Tom looked anxiously at his dad. He looked at him and saw... did Tom Sr. have tears in his eyes?

"I would count it a joy and privilege to meet your father," Tom Sr. said, blinking. "I'm sure I could learn so much from him and his lifelong ministry, as I have just come into this calling in the last few years."

April blinked, too. She seemed surprised by how caring, attentive, and genuine Tom Sr. was. Now, it was his turn to monologue: he explained his weekly routine and described his love for his family and community. But every now and then, she would glance warmly at Tom. He hoped he was measuring up, too.

April got an extra-long hug from Tom Sr. at the end of the meeting, and the two young people left for one more slice of small town adventure that Tom Jr. had been saving for the end of the afternoon.

They stopped by the Chicken Shack – his hometown's version of KFC - and picked up a barrel of chicken with biscuits and two sides. Their final destination was three miles out of town. As they arrived, it was the golden hour.

Tom led April to a grassy area along the bank of the creek that looked like it could have come from an altogether different time and place. It was so lush and green, it looked like no human had set foot there for fifty years. Tom had spent hours there as a child, and then as a teenager, alone with his thoughts.

"This is my place," said Tom.

"Our place," April added, nodding.

The two of them talked about things that didn't matter, ate cold chicken, and dreamed of a life spent always together. As they lay back on the wilting winter grass, the sun began to set, and April began to get colder. As she got colder, she cuddled closer to Tom, just as Tom had hoped she would.

April in his arms felt as warm as summer, and Tom didn't have a care in the world. Finally, everything was perfect.

When the two got home to Tom's parent's house, they found the elder Shoulds had just started a Christmas movie on the Hallmark Channel.

"I just made some popcorn with real butter," Tom's mom said with a knowing smile.

April smiled back at her.

Sitting on the couch with April felt like hearing his favorite song. Tom wanted to sing and dance wildly, but he kept quiet for the sake of those around him. Instead, he let his mind fast forward another year or two into what life could be like with April.

We could have it all, he thought.

He knew he could allow his mind to wander during the movie and still thoughtfully discuss the plot in an hour, because all of his Mom's Hallmark movies ended up in the same place.

A happy ending. A happily-ever-after ending!

Tom prayed that someday, he and April would have their happily-ever-after, too.

★★★

April was delighted to see this new side of Tom Should. He was more than just a scorekeeper, after all.

She loved how he paid attention to her this year, how he got excited when she tried something new instead of anxious like her father, how he was enjoying life - not just class rankings.

April was surprised to find that she preferred spending time with Tom Should to being at the top of the class.

Now that she had seen his family, his favorite things, his secret place - April felt she really knew Tom Should.

And she hoped that one day, maybe, she would be April Should.

***

New Year's Eve with all his family and his best girl by his side was mind-blowing. It gave Tom a glimpse of what was possible.

He had never imagined that anything could be so wonderful. As the Should family plus April watched the ball drop in Times Square, Tom knew what he should do.

Not today.

But someday.

He hoped she would say yes.

Chapter 9

That year, Tom was excited to get back to school in January. A new school year meant a new year with April - and a year closer to his career in communications. He imagined the things he would provide for April with the salary he knew he could achieve.

It was funny how the two really no longer cared what they majored in - only that they were together.

There were many late-night study sessions where both Tom and April's Christian roots were challenged. Yet by God's grace and believing in a future they had been raised to pursue, they stayed pure and only dreamed of a day where 1:00am would not mean goodbye.

Near the end of Tom's sophomore year, God decided that it was time for Tom Should Sr. to be called home.

It happened on a mid-May Sunday morning at about 7am. Tom Should Sr. was at his church office rehearsing the Sunday morning message when he felt his chest tighten.

He tried to call for help, but the only people in the building were two white-haired ladies laughing in the kitchen as they prepared communion for the congregation and Dixie cups of animal cracker snacks for the children's Sunday school classes.

It was Tom's mother who found his father slumped in his office chair with his head on the desk.

At first, she thought he was praying. But he wasn't.

He had gone to sleep preparing to preach about Jesus, and woke up to hear Jesus preaching!

At the funeral, Tom Should Jr. was in a daze. He listened to people applaud and praise his father, whose life had been so different from the one Tom Jr. was pursuing for himself. They all had such wonderful things to say about how his father had helped them. And Tom Should Jr. wondered what he should do.

He was so proud of his father and what he had become. But even in Tom Sr.'s passing, his voice was still loud in Tom Jr.'s head.

Son, Tom Sr. had said, before Tom Jr. went back to school, *You should be proud and take advantage of the education you're re-*

ceiving. Not everyone has that kind of opportunity. You are different from most people in this town. You are meant for something more.

What Tom heard when he played the voice in his head was: *You are* better *than everyone in this little town. Don't blow it!*

But was he really better than his father who had helped all of these people?

What should he do with his future?

Tom spent that summer at home with his mom. He kept selling cars and worked at a small furniture store because the radio station had shut down, just as Tom had predicted.

But he also began to work at the church in a way he had never expected.

On the second Sunday in June, his second Sunday in attendance, one of the elders asked if he would consider preaching the month of July. That would give the elders some relief and some time to carry out their search for a new pastor. This decision could not be made lightly, the elder explained. It was a long-term commitment – so it required a long-term search.

Tom discussed it with his mother, voicing his fears about whether he was capable of preaching, knowing that he'd never done it before.

"Tom," his mom said, "You're the best speaker I know. You know how to inspire people and get to the heart of a matter. I know you will make a great preacher. And it will reassure the people to see Tom Sr.'s son at the pulpit."

Tom knew his mom was right. He knew what he must do. He called the lead elder and accepted their assignment.

After all, it would only be for one month.

He spent the hottest month of the summer in between the furniture store and the air-conditioned church office sitting at his father's desk.

It felt strange to sit here. Nothing had been moved since his father's passing.

His father's books were still on the shelves, some of them pulled out and tilted sideways. Tom figured his father must have been referring to these in the last weeks of his life.

Tom would often touch the books and listen for his father's voice, imagining his father's fingers touching their smooth spines as well. Tom would often wonder what his father would do in his situation.

What would Tom Sr. say?

Tom remembered being told that his father's desk was very old and made of some exotic wood. The lacquer finish wore off long ago, which meant his father's coffee cups left rings where they were set. Tom stared at the pattern of rings as though it were a secret braille message from the other side. He would spend hours some days staring at the rings and straining to hear his father's voice in that office.

The old desk was also home to papers that were handwritten and barely legible, an open Bible, and a leather-bound day timer calendar full of future appointments that would never occur. Tom Sr.'s sports coat still hung on a cross shaped hook on the back of the door.

Each morning, walking into the office, seeing the coat and sitting in his father's chair, made Tom feel like there was a very thin space between him and his father. Perhaps that was why he spent so much time there – though he felt he did not make much progress on his sermons in that office.

Tom did not move anything in or out of the office during the month of July. It became a memorial. This place, so different from any he'd ever thought he'd work in, became his sanctuary.

Tom Should Jr. had a sharp mind, a love for the stage, and a strong desire to please God. Even if he didn't always know how to do that.

Tom did his best, searching the Bible for messages and leadership principles that seemed relevant to the congregation each week. Each week he was surprised when the words seemed to supernaturally enter his mind, and he found himself giving animated speeches to the congregation.

He was even more surprised when his messages earned enthusiastic applause and instant acceptance as the preacher of the small country church.

The last Sunday in July was bittersweet as Tom and everyone in the congregation knew his preaching assignment was over. He would soon be headed back East to college and to a very different life from the one his father had led.

After the message, Tom stood at the back door and shook hands with every last person. He fought back tears as he thought about what preaching had come to mean to him – he felt that every week he was helping these people. Giving that up and going back to pursuing sports cars and a house by the sea was surprisingly difficult.

Tom retired to his father's office and sat in his father's chair. He ran his fingers over the coffee rings on the old pastor's desk. He stared out the window at what his father had seen each time he sat in this chair.

He felt fulfilled and exhausted. It was the good kind of tired that comes with working hard to fulfill a meaningful purpose. He also felt an ache to be leaving it behind.

"I did it," Tom said quietly. "I'm still two months shy of twenty, and I preached a full month in a church! I think I could…" his throat tightened.

A knock on the door interrupted his reverie.

"Tom," a familiar voice said, opening the door a crack to peer inside.

Tom opened the office door to see seven people, all elders, standing in a tight circle in the hall beyond. They looked like a football team who had just broken from a huddle as they gazed at Tom expectantly.

"Can we talk to you?"

Tom welcomed the elders in and listened to an hour's worth of well-scripted reasons why Tom should remain in town and serve as an interim pastor of the small country church.

"We've been over it, Tom," the elders said, "and we just can't find anyone better."

Tom's heart soared. And crashed. What would happen to the future he'd promised April? She'd been clear that she didn't want to be a pastor's wife.

But...what about all the people around him? What about the elders who stood looking at him now?

Tom swallowed. He couldn't leave them behind.

If April loved him, she'd understand.

***

April was surprised when she got the phone call. But more than that - she was touched.

Her Tom putting aside his dreams of a high-rolling career and becoming a pastor like her father was the last thing she'd expected. But it showed something about Tom Should that was even more important than grades, or salary, or even hard work.

It showed compassion. Tom wanted to help those people more than he wanted a big house, or a fancy car, or a prestigious job title.

And April wanted that, too. She wanted a husband who cared about people more than promotions and prestige.

It seemed that she really had picked the right man when she had chosen Tom Should.

The next day, Tom moved the son's things into the father's office.

Tom did not return to the majestic buildings of his Ivy League school. He put his dreams of a degree in communications aside, and gained a seminary degree from an online college instead.

He continued to court April, who stayed at college. He promised he would never ask her to change for him, and that he still wanted kids and a wife who wrote books. She said she wouldn't want him to change for her, either. And that maybe, just maybe, she could get used to being a pastor's wife – if that pastor was Tom.

They were married two days after her graduation with a degree in Fine Arts. That was twenty years ago.

Chapter 10

Write your own chapter!

To participate in Tom and April's wedding visit: ***toddclark.org***

Hover over the **SHOULD HAPPENS** tab and click **THE WEDDING** link. Write your own version of their wedding, and read the versions that others have written for Tom and April.

Chapter 11

For a while, it seemed like Tom really had achieved his Hall-mark movie ending.

Being a pastor quickly became everything Tom had dreamed of. He may not have had a sports car, but he collected so much affirmation from those who saw him as carrying on his father's legacy. He got to use his gift for speaking and persuasion. And April seemed happy in the small town with a man who loved her for who she was instead of who everyone expected her to be. This cozy, bustling town was the ideal environment for her to write her books.

Tom had no regrets about his vocation. He soon felt he had been given the skills he had for a reason. It was to become the best leader this town had ever seen.

God blessed his years at his father's small church. In fact, church attendance grew so much that many people in his denomination said that he should start a new church – a bigger one than this town had ever needed.

Starting a new church was what every semi-successful, young entrepreneurial pastor should do, according to his peers and mentors. It was the sign of true success to create a community of people where there had been none before.

So he did.

He started a new church in the booming town of Green Springs, whose population was growing as the surrounding cities grew.

That was ten years ago.

Chapter 12

Back in the present, Tom needed an escape from his worries. He consumed a single IPA microbrew beer and embraced the only buzz that his Christian conscience would allow.

Tom's mind spun at a thousand miles per hour.

If he had come out to the mountains to be alone for noble purposes, this could have been considered meditation. But Tom realized this familiar sequence was not noble. He came here to compare himself to others, and that only led to his estimate of his own worth falling.

What should I do for my church?
What should I do for my family?
What should I do with my life?
How can I be the best?
Why am I not the best?
What should I do?!

For a moment, the mountain air allowed a new thought into his mind, and Tom realized he had been appropriately named. He laughed.

What should Tom Should do?
I love our city. And I love our church that will soon be ten years old.
But I also don't love them. I feel they're not what they should be. I don't think I can do this anymore.
Why? None of these blessings should make me feel so bad.

Tom quietly considered by name the small scaffolding of founding families who had invested their time and money in building the new church.

This had led to hundreds of other families joining, and that chain reaction set into motion a very driven church that matched perfectly the driven town of Green Springs. And the driven lives of

Tom and April Should.

Tom spent most of that Sunday night watching football on his cabin's small TV. It was a welcome escape from his world and a return to the life he'd known before, when he was a college student thinking only of his own success, unburdened by thoughts of work or family.

He spent Monday working on outlines for the coming Sunday's message that seemed far too close. "It seems like Sunday comes every 3 days," he thought as he stared for another ninety minutes at the skeleton outline he had for the coming weekend.

Tuesday morning came too early, and Tom drove from the mountains directly to the church office. He had gotten up late, so he missed his devotional time, but he felt that God should understand.

After all, Tom needed that energy for other things. He was going to the office to serve God and His church all day.

Margaret was pulling into the parking lot as Tom stepped out of his 1991 Honda Accord. "It's Tuesday, and you know what that means!" Margaret said with a big smile.

Margaret had no idea the pressure her suggestion applied to Tom's chest.

"I know," Tom said. "You'll have this weekend's outline by the end of the day," he smiled back, hoping his smile was just as wide.

Margaret could tell that the smile was fake, but she didn't know what to do about it.

As Tom began the familiar weekly struggle, he began to get angry.

This should be my favorite season of the year. It's four weeks until Christmas, he thought. *So why does everything feel like a burden? Why does every little thing feel like too much?*

Tom hurried to his office and sank low into the familiar old leather chair that he'd moved here from his father's office in the old country church.

The chair was only twenty years old, but he felt one hundred years removed from the dexterity of his youth, and his original purpose for entering this line of work.

To help people.

But now, he too often resented them. And he wasn't even sure why.

Everything he did was something he had once *wanted* to do. Everything he did was something he had once chosen. Everything he did was something he would choose again, if he imagined the scenario again.

But somehow, added all together, it was all too much.

Tom leaned sideways on the duct taped arm of the chair and turned on his laptop, seeking a distraction from his thoughts.

A couple dozen emails, each of them expecting a response. Each felt like a brick stacked on his chest.

Several new Facebook friend requests from new church members and first-time visitors. Each laden with expectations for what a pastor's social media presence should look like, how a pastor should interact with his congregants.

Then Tom's phone buzzed. That was the last straw. He almost threw it across the room.

Instead he took a deep breath, and slowly pulled it out of his pocket. He expected a reminder from April about some errand he needed to run, one more item on his to-do list.

Instead, his heart raced when he saw the name beside the text message: *Hank.*

"How are you doing, Tom? I'm praying for you today. Remember, I am your friend and fan. Call me sometime."

Tom looked at the text and thought about his friend.

Hank was an incredible and seasoned leader, widely regarded as a fountain of good advice for other young leaders. They'd first met several years ago when Tom had felt called to leave his father's church and plant a new church.

Tom and April had gone to meet with Hank to gain balance and wisdom during that transition season. Tom was feeling unsure about asking April to delay her writing career so that they could put all their energy into starting a new church.

Hank was like the 'most interesting man in the world' from

those beer commercials. He seemed to know everyone and had a story for everything. Yet somehow he still found time for people like Tom. Hank's guru status came from decades of counseling hundreds of leaders in both business and ministry roles.

"Call me sometime." Tom kept reading the text over and over.

He'd been hesitant to share his problems with anyone because, well – he was a pastor, and he was leading hundreds of people! Leaders were always supposed to know what to do. They were supposed to always be calm, to be endless fountains of wisdom. Like Hank.

How, Tom wondered, did Hank do it? The way everyone spoke about him, the way everyone wanted to spend time with him - Hank's to-do list must have been ten times longer than Tom's. Yet he handled it all with ease and grace, and he seemed to genuinely enjoy every minute.

Was Hank just made of sterner stuff than Tom?

This was not the first time Hank had sent a text asking Tom to call him. But in the past, Tom had been afraid of being a nuisance. Surely a famous leader like Hank didn't want to hear about Tom's personal problems. Did he?

Two rings were all it took, and Hank picked up.

"How's the successful megachurch pastor?" were Hank's first words. Tom could hear the jovial confidence in his voice, his certainty of Tom's success and the joy he took in it.

The kind greeting cut Tom to the heart. The next words out of his mouth were not what he had planned at all.

"I'm about done," Tom heard himself say. It was as though the weight that had descended on him was now spilling out of his mouth, through the phone, and onto Hank. Tom wanted to hold it back, but he just couldn't anymore. He needed someone to help him carry it.

"Great! Done with this week's message, and with five days to spare," Hank congratulated him. Always assuming the best.

"Not with the weekend message," Tom said, feeling his happily-ever-after collapse around his ears.

"I'm just about done with the ministry."

Part II: Meet Grace

Chapter 13

Hank was known for his ability to change people's lives.

He was twenty years older than Tom and seemingly ninety years wiser. He'd spent most of his life serving some of the most successful leaders in the nation, and in doing so he had gained for himself a reputation that was both respected and very well-compensated.

Hank's calendar was full. If you could get on it, you would pay his price with joy.

However, Tom and Hank's relationship was more about friendship than finances. Tom had chosen to focus on service over finance when he took over his father's country church, years ago. Tom and Hank each enjoyed the challenge, and the fresh eyes that the other provided.

For the next hour, Tom tried to unpack for Hank how he was feeling. It was a struggle: he'd always been afraid to share these feelings with those around him.

Hank listened for a long time, barely saying a word.

After nearly an hour had passed, Hank said:

"Should happens!"

Taken aback, Tom laughed. His friend always had a knack for constructing creative sentences, and Tom was his latest victim.

"Your life is uncommonly common," Hank pronounced. "Most people live their whole lives in the 'shoulds' without ever becoming aware of all the obligations they feel. These 'shoulds' silently direct their behavior, for better or worse, often without the person ever noticing. You're quite lucky to be aware of yours, Tom."

"So, I'm aware of my problem...but what should I *do* about it?"

"Well, let's start right there. You will have to change the way you think entirely. This takes time. Why don't we speak once a week for the next month?

"For this week, just go through your normal routine - observing and noting all the 'shoulds,' or obligations, that you feel as the week goes on. Try your best to make a list of all of them as you go through each day. You'll find it soon becomes impossibly long!"

"Okay, but then what?"

"Just make a list of them for now! And call me on Monday morning, when you're recovering from the weekend. We'll talk about the next step then."

"Is there really something we can do?"

Tom swore he could hear Hank smile. "There is so much you can do with this knowledge, Tom. I promise - you will be a new man by Christmas."

A new man by Christmas!

Tom agreed and hung up the phone with enthusiasm. His mentor's promise left him feeling lighter than he had in months. And maybe it was more than the promise: maybe simply saying how he felt had helped.

The message that afternoon flowed like it did that first summer twenty years ago. Everything seemed new.

Margaret was thrilled to have the weekend message outline on time, and April seemed surprised to have her husband truly home for a change. As he watched her blink in surprise at his laughter and his dad jokes, he wondered how much his son had noticed his absence - even when he was physically at home - over the past year.

The rest of the week was more productive than any he'd had in years. Tom felt he had the necessary mental margin to lead his staff, listen to new ideas, and even inspire several of his team members over long lunch meetings at the pizza shop.

It was a great week.

If only every week could be like this, Tom thought.

If Hank was right, maybe that could become a reality.

Tom hoped it would.

***

When Tom returned home with a new spring in his step, April was cautiously optimistic. She didn't ask what had happened; she didn't want him to close off like he so often did when she asked about his worries.

But when the joyful spring persisted for the rest of the week, when he smiled more and frowned less, April began to feel real hope.

Tom seemed to look at her more. He seemed to think about her more. She even caught him doing thoughtful little things around the house for her and Thomas. Being with Tom was a joy again, almost like it had been so many years ago.

But could it last?

April hoped it would.

Chapter 14

A week passed, and Tom was still walking on air.

The church was packed on Sunday morning, and the message that Tom had constructed was very well received. He felt a deep sense of satisfaction as he watched the people smile and nod to each other, leaving the church with lots of food for thought and prayer for the rest of the week.

But still, anxiety lingered in his mind.

Why can't every week be like this? He was already afraid that next week wouldn't be.

After spending a few hours at home Sunday afternoon, hurrying through the motions of relaxing with Thomas, Tom headed for his weekly mountain retreat.

The drive was easy, and the hairpin turns in the road leading up into the clouds were made for a sports car. The cabin sat at 6,000 feet, and the air nearly always felt cold, reminding Tom of his boyhood when his family would get in the car and adventure to find snow in the mountains at Christmastime.

Tom pulled his Honda into the driveway of his secluded little cabin and opened the door. It must have rained recently, because the smell of the pine trees was pungent and amazing. Tom felt transported to a completely different time and place. He grabbed a small Adidas duffle bag of clothes, a backpack with a few books, his laptop, and his journal.

Dropping the items on the cabin's bed, Tom quickly turned on the space heater and grabbed a familiar jacket out of the closet. Then he headed outside to begin his mile-high ritual.

He gathered pine needles from the forest floor first. Opening the cabin door with two hands completely full of brown prickly needles caused many of them to escape his grip and shower onto the floor between the door and the fireplace. The ones that made it through the fireplace's metal grating would be the base for his fire and serve the same purpose as paper kindling.

Then came small twigs, dry and rich in flammable sap. And finally, whole logs made from split tree trunks would be retrieved from under the sun-drenched and weather-beaten tarp that should really have been replaced months ago.

Starting the first fire on a Sunday night in the mountains was a treasured custom that fueled Tom's heart and filled his tank. The rich scent of pine smoke and the crackling of the logs as bright orange sparks shot out of them took him back to his boyhood days.

"There is no other place in the world that I should be," Tom said quietly.

With the fire blazing safely in its hearth, Tom felt the weight of the world drop from his shoulders. He laid down on the leather couch and drifted easily off to sleep.

As morning's first light snuck through the cabin window, Tom woke in the bedroom. He stretched lazily and wondered when he had left the couch after drifting off the night before. The thin walls of the mountain house were not a good guard against the cold, and Tom could see his breath misting in the morning light as he got out of bed.

He bundled up and stumbled into the kitchen, turned on the Keurig coffee maker and began to sift through the old coffee pods. All of the good flavors had been used months ago, and Tom again made a mental note to restock.

During his solitary morning coffee, a light sprinkle of rain turned into flurries of snow outside the cabin. Tom felt at complete peace as he picked up the cabin's landline and called Hank.

After only two rings, he heard his friend's familiar voice.

"Tom! How are you?"

They made small talk for about five minutes, but Tom could barely contain his excitement to hear what Hank had to say about his 'shoulding' problem. Finally, Hank said:

"Tom, get your journal. Find a blank page and write …

I should on myself when I …

Tom chuckled again, looking at the phrase on the page. But

then he turned serious. He had noticed all too well this week how bad the obligations he put on himself felt. He had noted more than a dozen before the end of his first day of recording his *shoulds*. Every one of them stressed him out and made him less present in the moment he was in.

Still, what could he do about them? He *should* do all of those things.

This is going to be difficult, Tom thought as he looked at the blank page that would soon be home to words that he hoped would cure his ailment.

Hank explained that they would spend the next three weeks talking about the "shoulds" Tom experienced in daily life.

"Let's start with what it looks like to should on yourself," Hank said.

Tom was silent.

"Tom," Hank continued, "I want to ask you a question. And I need an honest answer. Who are you trying to please?"

"What do you mean?" Tom asked, taken aback. He was a pastor. It was his job to please everyone. That's what pastors do: they serve and set a good example.

"I mean, *who are you trying to please* in your daily life?

"Who is your audience? Who do you hope will applaud you?

Tom thought about it.

He wanted Margaret to be pleased with his timely completion of his outlines, and with the way he led the church. He wanted *all* of his staff to be pleased with his leadership and oration skills. In fact, he wanted the whole *church* to be pleased with them. And with his family life, too. How could he speak to the congregation about his family life if it wasn't in good shape?

That left April and Thomas - the people he *should* have been trying to please - as almost an afterthought.

"Well," Tom ventured, "I know the *correct* answer. I *should* want to please God."

"That's the correct answer," Hank agreed. "But is it *your* answer?"

"Well...no. I guess not. I mean, it's there. But it's pretty far down my mental list. After pleasing everybody else."

"Good observation," Hank congratulated him.

"So...I guess I should just worry about pleasing God."

"Exactly."

"But what does that even look like? I'm not sure I know how to please God without pleasing everybody else."

"Do you believe your busyness pleases God?" Hank asked. "All the hours you spend stressing, does that please God?"

"No," Tom admitted. But the thought of laying aside all the busyness and stress felt impossible.

"Your distraction and your inability to be truly present with Thomas and April - do you believe that pleases God?"

"No. But how do I let go of it? They can't have a leader, husband, or father who is lazy and unproductive."

"So you should on yourself because you don't want to be seen as lazy?"

"Yes. Shouldn't we all avoid being lazy?"

"You will find that comes naturally when you have your priorities in order," Hank assured him. "Right now, you are staying busy out of fear. Fear of being seen as lazy. Fear of failing people. Fear of failing God.

"Why do you serve God?" Hank asked.

"Because I love Him." That answer was easy.

"And why do you serve the congregation?"

"Because...I love them?" Tom ventured.

"And Thomas and April?"

"I love them!" Tom exclaimed fervently.

"Exactly," Hank sounded satisfied. "You serve them because you love them. But you seem to have lost track of that truth. Instead, you now serve out of fear. You serve not out of love, but out of fear of not doing enough."

Tom contemplated this for a long moment. "Let me tell you a story," Tom said finally, "about a conversation I overheard between my mom and dad about twenty years ago.

"It was a Saturday night, and my mom had prepared a meal that was warm and ready to eat at 6:00pm. That was when my dad promised he would be done studying his Sunday message at church and be home to eat.

"Of course we knew that 6:00pm really meant at the earliest 6:30pm, and most likely more like 7:00pm.

"As 7:00pm passed I watched my mom make two plates of food for her and me to eat. And then I watched her clear the table of the place settings and put the remainder of the once-warm meal into plastic containers and into the refrigerator.

"It was another link in a string of Saturday nights where my mom and I ate dinner quietly in front of the television without my dad.

"An hour after we had cleaned our dishes, he showed up. His face looked wrinkled, and his shoulders pointed at the ground.

"'How is the message coming?' Mom asked cheerfully. Too cheerfully - I knew the cheerfulness was fake.

"'Ahh okay,' my dad sighed. 'I'm not sure it's very good. I should have spent more time on it this week.' But he glanced up at my mother guiltily. I could tell he felt he should have spent more time with us *and* with the message.

"We had heard this same narrative many times, but this time my mom's reply turned in a direction I didn't know she was allowed to go.

"'So, let me get this straight, Tom,' she asked with her false cheerfulness. 'You had all week to work on your message, but you did not get it done. So you worked tonight until past 8:00pm, and still have nothing but a mediocre message that you feel is 'Just OK.'

"As she said it, my dad looked like a schoolboy who was being scolded by his teacher.

"And then you missed a dinner that you told me you would be home to eat. Again.' Her voice was still cheerful, but it was also strong and firm.

"Mom had never said anything like this before! She was always patient and accepting of dad's busy life. I didn't know she was allowed to scold him the way she sometimes scolded me. I moved to the corner of the couch, out of the way, and watched to see how my father would respond.

"It was quiet for about 30 seconds. Then my dad said, very softly:

'Listen, I am doing the best I can. I am just trying to serve God!'

"'You are serving God with an inefficient work week, so-so sermons, and lack of quality time with your family?' mom asked.

When dad got mad, dad got quiet.

"He was quiet.

"For a long time."

Tom felt his throat go dry.

"I didn't know what would happen next."

Chapter 15

Tom couldn't believe he found himself sharing such a personal thing with Hank. Tom had always been the perfect one - the one everyone else came to for advice. Now he was spilling his deepest insecurities and fears. It felt scary.

But somehow, it also felt good.

"How did it feel," Hank asked Tom gently, "to hear your father go quiet like that?"

"I was scared," Tom admitted. "It felt kind of freaky to see them fight. I knew they both still loved *me*, but when they were angry with each other, it felt like anything could happen.

"'Tom,' my mom said. 'Why don't you go upstairs and work on your homework?'

"I didn't need to be asked twice to leave the room. That was the only time I could *ever* remember my mom or dad asking me to leave the room so that my parents could talk alone. As I left my mom hugged me, and my dad punched me in the arm. Both of them tried to look like nothing was wrong.

"I went to my room and shut the door. Then I laid down on the floor and put my ear up near the one-inch gap where the door hovered above the carpet. And I listened.

"I wondered if they would start screaming. I had a friend at lunch who talked about how his parents screamed a lot, and now they were getting a divorce.

"Most of what they were saying, I couldn't hear. But they weren't screaming, so I wasn't too worried. Just a little worried.

"I wondered what would change to stop my mom from being angry with my dad - or to bring my dad back into our lives.

"About 30 minutes into my espionage, when my ear had become finely tuned to the quiet words leaking under my door, I heard my dad yell.

"The volume caused me to lift my head off the carpet and scramble away from the door. As I sat in the middle of my room, I could hear my father's words loud and clear, thundering through the walls:

"Well, the devil never takes a break!"

"I don't know what was said between them after that. I just know it was quiet. My father went into the basement, and my mom went into the bedroom, and I let those words rush over me again and again.

"*The devil never takes a break.*

"I guess my dad figured that meant he couldn't take a break, either.

"I have lived with those words and that mindset for the past two decades," Tom said. "I can't take a break - because the devil sure doesn't."

Hank was quiet on the other end of the phone for long moments. "Thank you for telling me that story, Tom," he said at last. "And whether you realize it or not, you are helping me see the root of why you have spent so much of your life shoulding on yourself.

"Tom, the notion that the devil never takes a break is true. He does not. Neither does God.

"But God does not depend on us to do His will. His will will be done, no matter what we do. And He did not make us to do just one thing. If He did not want us to have families or enjoy life, He would not have made us with the capacity and desire to do so. He made creation to be enjoyed.

"Not everything that is true is noble. By setting your own life to a pattern of 'never taking a break' and living out that statement for all these years, you have actually made the devil your mentor."

It was horrible to contemplate, but making the devil his mentor...yes, that would explain why he'd been feeling this way for so many years.

"Just because something is true doesn't necessarily mean you should live by it. A simple truth like 'the devil never takes a break' is only part of the big picture. Christians are notorious for allowing half-truths to trip us up while ignoring bigger, more important truths."

Hank continued: "If you never say 'NO' to anyone's requests or expectations, and you believe you should care for everything, you will soon realize that you no longer care for anything!

"You have exhausted your capacity to care. One person saying 'yes' to everyone's expectations is like pouring water into the endless desert. It does not ultimately do anyone any good.

"The result of shoulding on yourself is that you will eventually *should* yourself to death!"

As Tom heard these words, he felt immense relief.

He didn't like hearing that he couldn't do everything - but at some level he had already known it. Now, it was an immense relief to hear that that was *normal!* Cutting off some people's expectations to spend more time with April and Thomas sounded like something he could do.

"Let me share with you just a short list of *shoulds* that we might think of as good. I wrote these down last night," said Hank. "These are all good things, and we would never say that any of them are untrue. But notice what happens when there are too many of them:

"You should be more loving.
"You should be more patient.
"You should be more motivated.
"You should pray more.
"You should be more generous.
"You should be able to do nothing and be OK with that.
"You should be productive.
"You should feel strong and confident at all times.
"You should never get angry.
"You should never waste time.
"You should declutter.
"You should take more vacations.
"You should spend more time with your kids.
"You should want to spend more time with your kids.
"You should have more fun.
"You should spend less time on technology.
"You should have more sex.

"You should want to have more sex.

"You should laugh more.

"You should make others laugh more.

"You should lose weight.

"You should exercise more.

"You should drink less.

"You should go on more dates with your wife.

"You should want to go on more dates with your wife.

"Your dates with your wife should be more creative.

"You should be happier.

"You should forgive.

"You should forget.

"You should move on!

"Even a list of good shoulds always ends in the same place: there are nearly infinite ways that you *should* be better. Now tell me, Tom, can you do anything *nearly infinitely*?"

"No," Tom admitted. "I can't do *anything* that much."

"The truth is," Hank continued, "there is simply not enough time in the day for you to do everything you think you should do. Even when they are good shoulds. Even when they might be true.

"If you try to do all of them, you will soon find you have no effort left to put into any of them! In your efforts to care for everyone and everything, you will soon find yourself not really caring about anyone or anything."

Hank's voice grew serious. "Let me ask you something, Tom. Do you ever feel numb? Do you ever know you *should* care about something, but you just can't care? Do you ever feel like you should feel more for your family…but you can't?"

"Yes," Tom replied, swallowing. *I feel like that all the time.* "I feel like I cannot care for all the things that I need to care about." It felt good to say it.

"Life is so unrelenting," Tom continued. "There's always one more ….

- Email to write
- Text to reply to
- Team member to align
- Call to return
- Book to read
- Coffee to schedule
- Lunch to drive to
- Message to research, write and deliver

Hank listened without offering a word. After a long pause, he dropped the bomb:

"I am not sure if you realize this or not, Tom, but life is so big and complex that you must actually steward your care and compassion. No one can care about everything or do everything.

"If we try, we end up doing nothing!"

Even Jesus did not have unlimited capacity to care.

"In your desire to do all the things you believe you should do, you have made the devil - not Jesus - your mentor. Your problem," Hank continued, "is something called *compassion fatigue.*"

"What's that?" asked Tom, frowning. It certainly sounded right, but he'd never heard of such a thing before.

"Compassion fatigue," Hank explained, "is the emotional stress, exhaustion, or apathy resulting from the constant demands of caring for others.

"Healthcare workers and leaders in the midst of startup businesses often experience it when they are surrounded by people who are in need all day. They simply become unable to care about anyone or anything if they do not rest or recharge, or if they try to solve everyone's problems. Pastors, entrepreneurs, and business leaders all experience this same human condition."

Moments like these were where Hank's 'guru' status shone. He could effortlessly move from small talk to unpacking significant ailments that Tom had never heard of, yet which seemed to be a perfect diagnosis.

"The needs of people never stop," said Hank. "So we assume we should not stop either. But then, what starts as compassion becomes a compulsion. A healthy organization needs many hands - not one person who never stops working. That won't end well for anyone."

"But you feel you cannot stop working. You are ruled by fear of what will happen if you do. Maybe you even feel that God's will being done depends on you, personally. Does that sound like something God would like you to think?"

"No," Tom admitted. And he felt a tremendous weight lifted from his shoulders.

"If even for a moment you consider not doing something – saying 'no' to something someone asks or expects of you - my guess is there is immediately a courtroom convened in your mind, where you put yourself on trial and present all kinds of evidence as to why you 'should' do this or that.

"Am I right?"

Tom was quiet.

"Yes," Tom said finally. "I have several common refrains that play in high definition in my head when I consider saying 'no' to someone or something. I am afraid of things like...

What if they don't invite us to dinner again?

What if they think we don't like them?

What if they decide not to invest financially because I didn't call or grab coffee?

What if I do go to lunch with them but then don't have time to complete my other obligations for the weekend?

"These fears drive me crazy, so I can't focus on anything I do. I am constantly convening a courtroom in my mind and shoulding on myself!

"Sometimes the shoulds shout, but most often they whisper to me."

"And the problem with the *shoulds*," Tom said, "is that they always make me feel like my current choice is the wrong choice. It's like a should is always sitting on my shoulder telling me what to do. And it never finds my choices to be right.

"So...what should I do?" Tom asked, opening one hand helplessly on the table, as though to receive wisdom.

"I need you to go *shouldless* for a while," Hank declared.

Tom stared at his hand. "That sounds hard," he said finally. His shoulds had always been with him. He couldn't imagine life without them.

"It is," Hank agreed. "But don't worry. I'll walk you through exactly how to do it."

Tom poised his pen over his paper and waited eagerly for Hank's next words.

If Hank was right, this could change everything.

What would the guru say?

Chapter 16

Hank allowed a long pause before he spoke again.

"Before you leave the mountains today," he pronounced, "I want you to make a 'to do' and a 'not to do' list for this coming week.

"The 'to do' list is what you *should* do this week, because there is such a thing as a helpful should. You just need to choose a handful of the most helpful shoulds and say 'no' to everything else, to ensure you don't run out of gas.

"Why don't you get started right now? Share with me what might be on the 'to do' list of noble or helpful shoulds."
Just thinking about choosing the right 'shoulds,' Tom began to get anxious. But he took a deep breath and closed his eyes. What was most important to his life?

- Loving my wife
- Spending time with my son
- Leading my staff
- Waking up early to exercise
- Eating a healthy lunch
- Reading for this weekend's message
- Writing this weekend's message
- Rehearsing this weekend's message…

As the list grew, so did the tightness in Tom's chest.

Abruptly, Hank asked: "How does that list of shoulds make you feel, Tom?"

"It makes me feel stressed. Like I should be more disciplined with my time if I actually want to accomplish all of those things. But…somehow, I can never seem to be. I can't focus, and everything takes longer than it should.

"My trouble is, I am not even sure there is enough time in the day to accomplish all the noble shoulds, let alone the non-essential shoulds that the courtroom of my mind holds me accountable for.

If I can't even do these things right, how can I possibly accomplish everything I should?"

"Exactly," Hank said.

Tom nervously touched his forehead.

"To accomplish any of them effectively, you have to limit your number of shoulds. Otherwise you will not be able to focus on or accomplish any of them. Choose a to-do list of no more than six shoulds for the week. Consider these the 'big rocks' that you choose to fill your life. Everything else will just have to fit in around them.

"And then make a not-to-do list of things that are important - but aren't urgent and don't need to be accomplished this week.

"You might be surprised to find that these not-to-dos get done even faster when you are really focused on your to-dos in the moment and are no longer distracted by dozens of other to-do list items."

Hank paused. "Tom," he said, "remember, if you want to get your to-do list done, you are going to have to give yourself permission to say 'no.' Permission to *not* do anything that isn't one of your big rocks."

Tom tried to imagine saying, "no" the next time an unexpected business matter, or invitation, or request came up. He tried to imagine saying, "I'll take care of that later," or delegating the task to someone else.

It felt scary. His mind filled with possibilities of bad things that might happen if he said,

"no."

It felt scary, but it also felt incredibly liberating, like a huge weight was lifted from his shoulders, and he could finally breathe again.

"Grace is the antidote to shoulding on yourself," Hank said, after giving Tom a long moment to consider what he'd said. "You see, every should carries an insidious message: 'If you don't do this all perfectly, you are an imperfect person.'

"Well, of course we're imperfect! If we were perfect, we'd all be the same! There's only one perfect person, after all - and that's Jesus.

"Jesus came to set us free from a life of 'shoulds.' He became the perfect sacrifice so that we wouldn't have to be. Jesus showed that he loved everyone - no matter what 'shoulds' they were or were not meeting.

"In fact, he hung out more with people who had broken a lot of 'shoulds' but who had love in their hearts than he did with those who followed every letter of the law and had no love for anybody.

"Some view Christianity as a way of life built on shoulds - built on striving for perfection. We often tell ourselves we should love others, we should be more generous, we should serve more, and the list goes on.

"Some of the shoulds of faith are experienced as positive and uplifting: this is a great source of pleasure. When we do what's right, we feel good about ourselves and feel that life has meaning and purpose.

"But when we do not do what we should do, we feel bad, guilty and unworthy. And that makes it even harder to love ourselves or others as Jesus did.

"When we embrace every 'should' that whispers in our ear, we can even end up hating ourselves and others because we feel we fall short.

"That isn't what Jesus wants. He wants us to live from a place of love - not just a place of following the rules.

"So next time you find yourself thinking, 'I *should* do this, ask yourself: 'If I do this, will I have love left for my wife? For my son? For other people?'"

Tom thought about this.

"Jesus never denied that there are things we should do. There are good shoulds.

"But He also showed what happens when we get caught up in the wrong shoulds - the shoulds that become *more important* to us than the love that *should* motivate us. The things we feel we have to do because we *should* - not because it is loving toward anybody.

"And this is where the perfect life intersects with the sacrifice of Jesus and sets us free and takes us back to grace.

"He shows that we *should* be motivated by love, and when we're not, we're being motivated by something else. Maybe by fear of not accomplishing all our 'shoulds.'

"When you get back home this week," Hank advised, read Matthew 11:28-30. "And please give some forethought to your schedule.

"Remember, opportunity does not equal obligation. If you say 'yes' to every should, you will soon run out of love for the ones that really need your love."

"Ah," Tom said, "I like that." It was easier to consider saying 'no' to invitations and requests when he saw that it was *really* saying 'yes' to what was most important.

**Opportunity does
not equal obligation.**

I think this is why I should on myself, Tom thought.
I see every opportunity as an obligation.
I see every invitation as an investigation or commentary on
my commitment, on whether I care enough about a person
or cause. But it's not my job to care about everything.
And when I try, I end up not caring about anything!

"Yes," Hank repeated. "Just because you can do something, does not mean you should!"

Hank chuckled. "You come from a long line of 'Shoulds.' I mean, think about your dad and his life. How he did what he should do throughout his life.

"His life was full of 'good' shoulds, Tom. But sometimes those shoulds left out things that were pretty important, didn't they?"

"Yes," Tom said quietly.

"You are literally a second, third, fourth, fifth generation 'SHOULD.' I bet if you went back and learned more about your dad's dad and his dad…you would see a pattern of good and not-so-good shoulds! The shoulds run deep in most families."

After another twenty minutes of freedom-laced small talk, Tom promised to make the two lists Hank requested and to call again next Monday. The two friends said goodbye.

As Tom hung up the phone, he looked around his little cabin.

It looked new, fresh, exciting. He let out a long sigh.

"I think I might survive!" he declared to the cabin walls.

No one heard him speak, and that was what he liked about the cabin. He could speak openly to the trees all that was often quarantined within the quiet recesses of his mind.

The cabin felt like a place where he could be truly free - without worrying about what he should say to others. At the cabin he felt more real than he felt rehearsed, and that felt good.

He wished he could feel like this all the time. But was that really possible?

Chapter 17

As Tom descended the mountain and approached Green Springs, he really did feel like a new man. Full of energy and vigor, he decided to stop by the local high school and surprise his friend Vance.

Vance was the local high school principal. He had joined the church two years earlier, and he and Tom quickly became friends. Vance and his family had lived in the town for generations, and he remembered every student he was responsible for. So whenever Tom needed to know about a new family or the history of an old-timer, Vance was sure to be full of insights.

Tom pulled into the school parking lot, which was now almost empty after school hours. But he knew Vance would be in his office, looking over administrative work and making sure everything was perfect.

Walking through the empty halls filled with lockers reminded Tom of his own youth, so many years ago. His footsteps echoed on the linoleum until he reached the heavy wooden door of the principal's office, knocked, and waited for the muffled: "Come in!" from inside.

Vance's office was like a museum. The bookshelves held books that were first used by his great-grandfather and now held time-honored places. The walls were adorned with old, flimsy 8x10 frames that contained the degrees of three generations of his family. Vance was born to be an educator and destined to be a principal. Tom remembered sitting down at his own father's desk, so many years before.

As Tom caught a glimpse of himself in one of the glass frames, he realized that he looked like an unshaven mountain man returning from his weekend retreat. He smiled at the mental image of himself as any sort of wild man.

"How are you?" he asked Vance, looking at the principal in his dress shirt and slacks. Vance always looked like he was in charge - but also like it wasn't easy.

"Is it Friday yet?" replied Vance with an exhausted grin that resembled a wince.

Tom offered his best attentive smile and sat down in the chair before Vance's desk. The man clearly needed someone to listen.

Vance sighed, shaking his head at what he called Tom's 'pastor posture.' "I just feel like Mondays are more of a chore than they used to be," he spilled. "I remember when I first got my degree and started teaching, it all seemed so magical. I was helping kids become adults. Good adults, I hoped.

"Then being promoted to become the assistant principal at my alma mater - it seemed like a dream. Now I'd be responsible for all the young people's education, and I was going to give them the best I could.

"But the last four years as principal have felt like fourteen years. I know this is what my dad and his dad did, but sometimes it seems like life was simpler back then. Green Springs was smaller. So were people's expectations."

It was all Tom could do to be quiet and listen. Everything in him wanted to enlighten Vance with the knowledge of his common hidden ailment, of his feelings that mirrored Tom's own.

But Vance needed the same thing Tom had needed at first: for someone to just listen. For someone to listen to the feelings he felt he couldn't tell his students or his family.

And Tom himself had only really begun to understand his own problem seven hours ago.

I need to live this before I give this.

Tom knew he had a propensity to get enamored with new knowledge and share it before it had been lived out and become wisdom. He could hardly expect to be an expert in something he'd never done himself!

Being quiet was hard for Tom. Every part of him wanted to encourage Vance and tell him it would be fine. But he knew where Vance stood: it didn't *feel* fine, and people telling him that would just make it feel like they didn't understand. Like they weren't listening.

So Tom held his words. For now.

The two talked for another 40 minutes about a cafeteria food fight that resulted in three suspensions and how Green Springs traffic was becoming unbearable. Vance worried about the kids just learning to drive in such a busy and congested city, and Tom listened to all of his concerns.

Near the end of their conversation Vance asked Tom if he and April would like to meet for dinner or drinks on Friday night. Tom was actually open and willing to go, but even more excited to try saying 'no.'

"No, I am sorry," said Tom. "April and I will not be able to meet this Friday. We are staying home together to watch a movie." This was a plan Tom was making on the spot that he would need to be sure to share with April.

Ha, I did it!

One 'no' already spoken, and it's only Monday afternoon, Tom thought proudly to himself.

When Tom arrived home at 5:10pm, he was fifty minutes early for dinner, and April was thrilled.

So was Tom. He felt lighter than he had in years, and overflowing with love to give her.

That night, Tom told April at length about his conversation with Hank. He gushed about how the mountains were definitely a thin space, where the distance between himself and God seemed to shrink.

"Why do you think you should on yourself so often?" April asked, watching Tom with concern. Tom wondered if she had the same problem - though he'd been too wrapped up in his own shoulds to notice.

"Well," he shrugged his shoulders and sighed, "I believe I have this compulsion to work. That's what my dad and his dad were all about. Hard work equals success. And just shutting down, being together, not striving for anything - they didn't really do that.

"It is so hard for me to shut down and just enjoy where we are as a family. And it is crazy because after years of living on purpose we have tremendous favor at work, great friendships, family, and margin in our finances. We are at a place that most people only dream about.

"But I can't seem to enjoy it because I'm always trying to get to an even *better* place. I'm always trying to get somewhere else. I've spent my whole life feeling I should do everything and getting upset when I can't. Feeling that I should care for everything. And now when I try to pull back … I can't."

As he spoke, Tom felt his throat tightening. A few hours ago on the mountain with Hank, it had seemed so simple. But now that he sat back in the family home he'd worked so hard to build, the overwhelming weight of all the shoulds he felt came crashing down on him. How could he possibly rid himself of all of them?

Tom took a deep breath. "I mean, I can stop for a little while. But almost immediately my mind tells me I am being lazy, and I should be operating at the same speed I have operated for the past 20 years. I should always be going and going. I should always be somewhere else."

April nodded sympathetically.

"Oh, another thing," Tom remembered suddenly. "Hank told me something crazy: I have made the devil my mentor!"

"What?" April exclaimed, ready to defend her Tom. "I can't think of anyone who's more vigilant…"

Tom nodded enthusiastically, smiling. "Exactly!" he explained. "The devil wants us to be afraid. When we're driven by fear, we're not driven by love. So when I'm driven by fear of not doing enough or being good enough," he reached for April and held her tightly, feeling fear replaced by love, "then I can't be here. With you. Because I'm not being driven by love. I'm being driven by fear."

April melted against him, and he thought he heard tears in her voice. "Oh, Tom."

Tom continued, "I have bought into the lie that since the devil never takes a break, I should never take a break. And because of that, I've been sapping myself of the love I want to give to you and Thomas and even the people of Green Springs."

Remembering that these shoulds could be tools of the devil, even if they were good shoulds, liberated Tom. It gave him the permission he needed to put them aside.

Tom recounted the whole story of being asked to leave the room and hearing his mom and dad arguing as a teenager. April held him tightly and listened.

"I can't care for everything," Tom finished, quietly. "When I try, I'm left with no love to give to *anything*.

"I am so sorry, April. I am sorry for how my drives and motivations have been off course. I've been trying to do God's good work, but I've been doing it out of fear, not love. And I know that you and Thomas have felt that keenly.

"My fear of not being good enough, of not doing enough, has caused me to should on myself nearly every moment of our marriage for the past twenty years. I would have told you if I had understood what I was doing. But I just thought I was doing what I should, and I didn't understand why I felt so distant all the time.

"I thought one day I would read the right book and gain insight into the perfect schedule that had been alluding me. I thought I just wasn't doing enough, not that I was doing too much.

"I thought better time management would bounce me out of this mental circus, and then I would be able to do *everything* I should. Or I might come across the right scripture, and I would gain spiritual dexterity that would allow me to do what I should without constantly putting myself on trial over whether I was doing *enough*."

He stopped and took a deep breath. "Anyway, I'm sorry, April. With Hank's counsel, I am going to try to make a change."

April nodded softly against his chest.

Tom held that moment and treasured it for a long moment.

But then his mind leapt ahead, to how much better he would be at the office tomorrow. Without the weight of all his shoulds, he would get more done than ever before.

He almost didn't hear April say: "Don't forget, tomorrow is Thomas's soccer fundraiser. It's at 4:30, so I won't be cooking dinner. We'll be eating with the team and bidding on items to fund the team's summer travel schedule."

"Sounds good," Tom agreed.

But his mind was already somewhere else.

Chapter 18

When his phone alarm vibrated on the bedside table at 6:00am, Tom woke up without one snooze tap. He felt ready to tackle his to-do list and was sure he would bulldoze it all within a few hours.

This was the first time in years that Tom felt so free and full of energy.

The coffee that morning tasted extra good, and Tom grabbed a cereal bar to take to the office. He quietly kissed April on the hand and headed out the door.

I remember when we first started this new church , Tom thought to himself as he drove into the church parking lot, seven short miles from his home.

I was full of ambition and purpose. I'm sure I overestimated what we could do in a few years and underestimated what we could do in a few decades.

Tom got out of his car and closed the door, looking at the empty parking lot around him.

I've imposed too many shoulds on those around me. I should on them just like I should on myself.

Tom pulled out his keys and opened the church lobby doors. It was quiet inside. And dark.

It had been quite a while since Tom had been here before the sun.

Sitting at his desk, Tom pulled out his journal and looked at the list that Hank had asked him to create.

What should I do today?

What should I *not* do today?

I should encourage my team, Tom thought. *I must lead them well and make sure they feel valued.*

An hour passed as Tom worked on his shoulds until the sun was peering through the bookshelves and spilling onto Tom's office desk.

Tom got on his knees and began to talk to God.

Thank you, God, for this morning.
Thank you for my family and friends.
My wife and son.
And this church and team I get to lead.
Father God, thank you for exposing my unhealthy appetite to
should on myself. I know you accept me just as I am.
I know that comparing people, and deciding what they're
worth, is wrong.
It's the opposite of what you taught us to do.
Father God, please help me to have only you as my
audience. Forgive me for trying to please everyone.
And forgive me for spending more time building my kingdom
than yours.
I know there are only two kingdoms I can build.
Help me to follow your promptings today and build your
kingdom, leaving mine far behind.
Show me, God, how to quit living in the shoulds that rob
freedom and subject me to fear.

Tom thought he heard a noise somewhere in the building and looked up. He tried to close his eyes again to pray, but too many scary movies and evening news clips ran through his head.

Who else could be at the building at this early hour? A team member, or a murderer!

Tom grabbed the baseball bat he kept behind his desk and headed down the hallway toward the conference room.

"Hello?"

Not a sound.

He crept into the conference room, reaching a hand in to turn the light on as a warning. "Hello?!"

It was now 8:35am, so it was not impossible that a staff member had come into work. But outside the conference room windows, the parking lot was empty.

So was the church, as Tom inspected it painstakingly, room by room.

With a deep sigh, Tom went back into his office and opened his Bible to the book of Galatians.

I really am driven by fear, he thought.

It's time for a fresh start.

Chapter 19

Tom knew that Galatians was the book to go to. The apostle Paul had chided Galatia's people: *justification is not through the law, but through Christ.*

Justification came not from shoulds, but from love and grace, Paul said.

Even 2,000 years ago, just a few years after Jesus had been with them in person, Christians had begun to forget that. As Tom began the first chapter, he murmured to himself:

"It's been a long time since I read the Bible to gain wisdom for my own life - not just to dispense to someone else."

This is what I should be doing early every morning, Tom decided, and mentally committed to it.

Ask Tom began to read, he realized that the new believers in Galatia also suffered from a serious case of the shoulds.

They had been taught about Jesus.

They had put their faith in Him.

They had received grace.

Yes!

They had moved from the should life to the good life.

But they quickly went back to living the same old shouldy way.

They went back to imposing laws and standards on themselves instead of resting in grace.

They went back to living in fear.

Tom read in Galatians 1:6, *"I am astonished that you are so quickly deserting the one who called you to live in the grace of Christ."*

Paul was astonished! These people were given the opportunity to live in the grace of God's perfect acceptance of them. They didn't have to should on themselves. And for some reason, some unimaginable reason, they were giving up living in grace and returning to a life of fear and shame.

Why do we do that? Tom wondered.

As he entered Galatians Chapter 2, he found his answer.

"This matter arose because some false believers had infiltrated our ranks to spy on the freedom we have in Christ Jesus and to make us slaves." - Galatians 2:4

Wow, Tom thought, *the shoulds are sneaky.*

Shoulds are *'spying on my freedom,'* Tom noted in his journal. Then he began to speak aloud, preaching to himself:

"So there were people who said they were followers of Jesus, but they weren't. They didn't understand grace, and grace is the heart of Christianity. They wanted to put the shoulds that Jesus had taken off the Galatians back on the Galatians. They judged people and tried to outdo each other. They acted out of evil, out of fear of not being good enough, instead of out of love.

Wow, Tom thought, *this is half of my church.*

And I have not helped. I have should on myself and others. That has been the behavior I've modeled, the example I've set for those I lead.

I have accepted Jesus into my life. He has saved me from my sins. He has removed the guilt, shame, striving and comparison. He brings me freedom. He teaches unconditional love. He vanquishes the shoulds from my life.

But instead of living in freedom...I begin to re-introduce a new series of shoulds.

"I should all over myself!"

"I will preach this someday," Tom said excitedly to himself. For the first time in months, he felt truly inspired as a sermon began to form in his mind.

"But aren't there good shoulds?" He paused, reflecting. "There *are* some things that surely we should and should not do."

"The problem is, I can't live up to all of them!

"I just can't do it.

"And when I try - I don't live up to any of them.

"It puts an impossible burden on me.

"And then I transfer this same burden to my family, friends and congregation."

Tom continued reading, seeking the answer to this dilemma. Then, near the end of Galatians Chapter Two, he read:

"For when I tried to keep the law, it condemned me. So I died to the law – I stopped trying to meet all its requirements – so that I might live for God. My old self has been crucified with Christ. It is no longer I who live, but Christ lives in me. So I live in this earthly body by trusting in the Son of God, who loved me and gave himself for me. I do not treat the grace of God as meaningless. For if keeping the law could make us right with God, then there was no need for Christ to die."

**Jesus died so I wouldn't have
to live a shouldy life.**

"If I keep living the old way, why did Jesus even die for me?" Tom said to his empty office.

"Jesus didn't come just to remove our sins; He came to remove our burdens. He wants to teach us a new way of life where we learn not to should on ourselves.

"It's the way of grace.

"Grace," Tom heard himself say, "is humble and easy and light. Grace means I don't have to live up to the standards of this world. I don't have to place a high price tag on myself or devalue others who don't share my priorities.

"I can fall short of my own standards, and not be perfect and always producing, and that's okay." Tom tasted the words on his tongue. "I'm still loved and still accepted. That's how God is. My position with God is not determined by my performance. And there is nothing I could *do* to make God love me any more or any less."

Tom took a deep breath.

"I can be truly free," he pronounced to himself, "of the shoulds that come from constant comparison."

Comparisons are killing me, he thought to himself.

Tom suddenly remembered the verse he learned twenty-five years ago at summer camp from Paul's letter to the Corinthians:

"Of course we would not dare classify ourselves or compare ourselves with those who rate themselves so highly. How stupid they are! They make up their own standards to measure themselves by, and they judge themselves by their own standards!"

Tom felt guilty for a few moments about his propensity to compare. But then he gave himself some grace.

Part of the problem, he realized, was that it was easier today to compare yourself to others than ever before. Today everyone seemed to know thousands of people, and all of them had houses, cars, salaries, awards, skills, and virtues to measure yourself against.

"It's about time we admitted that our constantly connected world is like a petri dish for comparisons." Tom tried the words on, imagining speaking them to his congregation.

"Here is what we do: we look at our friends on Facebook and Instagram where everyone presents the best versions of their lives. We watch them share the new stuff they are buying and great things they are doing. We look at our towns, schools, and businesses which are full of thousands of people, and we tell ourselves, *I should be the best.*"

"We feel like we should live up to impossible standards.

"We should have those things.

"We should go to those places.

"We hear about our friend's kids. How they're playing baseball, and basketball, and soccer, and learning karate, and taking cello lessons, and they're in the junior baking championship, and what is going on? What's wrong with my kid? My kid is learning how to clean his room, and the only contest he could enter is for making fart noises."

Tom smiled to himself. "We think, 'my kid should be better, should be smarter, should be in more activities.'"

"It's like we're competing in an unwinnable race."

"It's not winnable," Tom said, to his empty office, "and it's not even the race we are supposed to be running. Jesus didn't tell us to be rich, or smart, or get trophies, or wear stylish clothes. He told us to love one another. And that's exactly what we don't do when we're shoulding on ourselves. We don't even love ourselves."

"So, what's the solution for shoulding on ourselves?" and Tom remembered Hank's words.

He turned in his Bible to Matthew, Chapter 11.

"Are you tired? Worn out? Burned out on religion?
Come to me. Get away with me and you'll
recover your life. I'll show you how
to take a real rest.
Walk with me and work with me—watch how I do it.
Learn the unforced rhythms of grace.
I won't lay anything heavy or ill-fitting on you.
Keep company with me and you'll learn
to live freely and lightly."

By the time Tom was done reading Galatians, it was nearly 9:45am. There was still not a soul at work at the office.

Where is everyone?

I can't believe no one is here working at nearly 9:45am.

Tom's mind skipped past the fact that most days he arrived at half past nine.

This is crazy.

I mean, this church pays its staff to be here.

To work.

To serve.

To get things done!

And without even knowing it,
Tom began to should all over his team.

I think what we need is office hours, Tom thought, *a period of time each day where people* have *to be here.* He began to type an email on his computer that his team should receive as reasonable.

But as Tom was typing, he heard laughing.

Tom looked outside and saw his whole team- all eleven staff

members - arriving at the same time. He rushed to the lobby, prepared to demand answers about where they'd been.

But before he could speak, his executive pastor said warmly, "We missed you at breakfast, Tom!"

Breakfast.

"Oh yes, I know," Tom lied. He had completely forgotten that this was the single morning each month when the team had breakfast together before work.

Every first Tuesday the team reserved a room at Denny's. This was something that Tom had heard about a leader doing years ago and then instituted for his team. Not because he wanted to, but because the communicator on stage at the conference made it seem so synonymous with team health.

I'll have the best team, Tom had thought. *I'll use his technique of team breakfasts.*

Tom had led the first three months' meetings, but then handed it to his executive pastor and had not attended himself in nearly a year. He felt he was too busy. There were too many other things he should be doing.

"Of course," Tom said, covering his earlier anger with a bright smile. "How was breakfast? A grand slam, I hope!" Everyone laughed.

"It was great," said Margaret, "but you really should join us sometime, Tom!"

From there on out, Tuesday ran smoothly. Tom interacted with grace and humor with his staff then retreated to his office. He was being so productive that he skipped lunch and felt good about it.

All the emails are sent, and an outline for this weekend's message is ready to roll! I'll be home before 5:00pm! He thought triumphantly.

Tom was thrilled with his progress.

As he walked down the staff hallway at 4:30pm, he noticed that only three of his eleven staff were still working.

Hmm, he thought. *Nearly everyone is checked out before 5:00pm, and they didn't start until 11:00am. Maybe we do need those office hours after all.*

But he felt so good about his accomplishments today, nothing could bother him much.

Pulling into the garage at home, Tom felt free.

It had been a good day.

"Hello!" he announced himself, striding into the family kitchen. Tom frowned. The house was empty and quiet. It echoed in a way it only did when no one else was home.

"Hello?" He checked upstairs.

I wonder where everyone is?

Tom finally returned to the kitchen, and that was when he found the note from April:

We are at Thomas's soccer fundraiser at Pizza Barn.
I hope you remembered. I hope you can come.

Love, April

Tom felt panic rising in him as he turned and bolted for the garage.

Chapter 20

April stared straight ahead, keeping a smile fixed on her face as she drove Thomas to the Pizza Barn. In the back seat, Thomas twisted to look out the window at the cars that whizzed past.

She knew what he was thinking: *Where's dad? Is he coming?*

She was disappointed, but not surprised when 4:00pm came and there was no sign of Tom. This had become the norm: he was too wrapped up in his work to remember his family life.

She wondered why it hadn't been like that for the first few years of their married life. She wondered what had changed.

Maybe it didn't matter, she thought as she rounded a corner.

Maybe it didn't matter why Tom had changed. Only that he had.

★★★

The judge banged the gavel, and the echo reverberated inside Tom's mind as he jogged for the garage, fumbling in his pocket for his car keys.

Court was in session again.

How could you forget the most important things in your life? Tom demanded of himself, staring angrily down from the judge's bench. *Even with Hank's help, you are still failing to fulfill even your most important shoulds.*

I can make it! Tom thought frantically as he sped out of the driveway and pulled into rush hour traffic. It was like the whole city was trying to get home, and everyone lived on the same street.

Where is everyone going?

Are you kidding me?

"Damn it," Tom swore out loud. He instantly regretted it, but how could he have been so caught up in his own world that he missed the lives of the people around him?

The dam inside him began to break as Tom drove toward Pizza Barn: he should on every person he passed.

They should move faster.

They should have taken a different route.
They should have turned before the light changed.

By the time he pulled up in the parking lot, he had actually convinced himself that it was April's fault he had forgotten. She should have called to remind him.

As Tom rushed into the restaurant with a hurried, apologetic smile, his eyes met April's. Her gaze was cold, and his quickly turned to ice.

How could she have let me forget?

That night at home, it was a challenge to smile as the two put Thomas to bed and said his prayers. April's look, as she rolled over and went to sleep, said it all.

She had thought, briefly, that something was going to change for the better, but she didn't think that anymore.

Wednesday was meeting day at the office, and Tom didn't have time to should on himself or anyone else. There was barely enough time in the day to bounce from meeting to meeting about the potential new satellite church campus site, its new billboard, and finances. Tom was ten minutes late to nearly every gathering.

Why does Margaret schedule these meetings so close together? Tom wondered, as he walked to his car at the end of the day. *Maybe I need a new assistant who understands the pressures I am under.* Then he stopped and looked at his ride.

A ten-year-old, beat-up Accord.

Really?

I work so hard and this is what I have to drive?

Looking around the parking lot Tom took a mental inventory of all the Landrovers, BMWs, Mercedes, and Porches that poured into this church parking lot every Sunday morning. It seemed like every person he knew had a car that would be fun to cruise, except him.

Tom's blood was boiling by the time he got home.

"Hello!" he called with false cheerfulness. When no one answered, it was almost a relief. "Is anyone home?" He tried again, tentatively.

I wonder what they're doing now, he thought angrily.

It was 8:00pm before Tom saw the note on the kitchen table

from April about the program at school.

"*Please call me when you get home,*" the note said.

Mixed emotions boiled in Tom as he read it.

On one hand, he was frustrated that he felt April had once again failed to communicate.

But at the same time, he had been so eager to blame someone else for his unmet expectations that he hadn't even thought to look for a note.

✦✦✦

April sat at the Awards Ceremony, watching bright lights highlight each student as they walked forward to accept their trophy. She waited patiently for Thomas's name to be called, but part of her mind was somewhere else.

Love and frustration resided in her mind, both toward Tom. She was so frustrated that Thomas was missing his father as he grew up. She could have put aside her own sadness that Tom rarely seemed to see her anymore, but Thomas growing up with a father who was barely there was something else entirely.

And a new worry was growing in April's mind. Tom seemed so stressed all the time. He seemed overworked. The way he rushed from place to place; she worried about his health.

He didn't even seem to sleep anymore. Most evenings, he came to bed after her. Most mornings, he was gone before she woke.

I understand his drive, April thought quietly. *It lives inside of me, too. But now it seems that our priorities are different. I wonder if he realizes how much I do.*

Does Tom realize how I bring in extra income, to help Thomas go to all his classes and summer camps?

Does he realize how I do almost all of the cooking and cleaning, so that he doesn't have to?

Does he realize how I listen to his troubles at the end of the day, when he hardly ever asks about mine?

Does he remember how we used to compete and that I can do just as much as he can? Does he remember that I could just as easily have had that prestigious job if I hadn't chosen to marry him? If he hadn't chosen to devote all of his time and energy to his career?

April felt like her work and talents were invisible to Tom and to the world. If she ever stopped doing that work, she knew Tom's world and work would fall apart within a few days.

But Tom seemed to have forgotten that. He only seemed to see the things she didn't do.

I wish Tom would see me as a partner in his endeavours.

I bet he has no idea how much time I spend each day, working to support him.

April's mental courtroom adjourned when she heard her son's name pronounced.

She burst into wild applause and simultaneously scrambled to remember what it was her son had won.

★★★

Tom felt terrible on many levels as he selected April's number on his cracked smartphone screen.

"Hello! Are you OK?" April's voice on the other end was anxious.

"Yes," Tom sighed heavily. "I'm fine. I had a bad day. Sorry."

"Oh thank goodness," he heard relief flooding her voice. "I was so worried about you when you didn't show up at Thomas's award ceremony." Her worry had apparently supplanted any anger she might have felt. "We'll be home in ten minutes. Do you need me to pick you up anything to eat?"

"No thanks, I'm good," Tom said, as his eyes stung and filled with tears.

Tom met the car as it pulled into the driveway. Trying his best to keep his composure, he apologized to April and to Thomas. "I've just...had a hard day," he said. It was a relief to say that, instead of trying to insist that he'd been right and someone else had been wrong.

"It's okay, Dad," Thomas said, hugging him. "Everyone makes mistakes." Tom's eyes teared up again as Thomas said this.

His family was resting in grace.

His family was choosing a good life rather than a should life.

And Tom suddenly felt like, with all his shoulding, *he* was the one who was being left behind.

That does it, Tom thought.

I am better than this.

I am going to do it.

I am going to live in grace if it kills me.

It occurred to him that that attitude might not be in the spirit of grace, and he switched gears.

I am going to live in grace, he thought, *for April and Thomas.*

Chapter 21

On Thursday, it was time for Tom to lead his team and navigate work again.

How could he do what he should without shoulding on himself and others?

As everyone filtered into their offices on Thursday morning, Tom decided to lead by walking around. One of the things on his to-do list was to love and lead his team better and engage with them more.

"How are you?" Tom asked as he stepped into his worship pastor's office.

Lance flipped around in his chair, looking surprised. "I'm doing great, Tom!" His face burst into a grin. "I'm so excited about this weekend. I have a great worship team in place. We are rehearsing tonight, and my son just made a select soccer team!

"My wife is doing very well in her new job, but I should let you know" - he paused, anxiously, looking to Tom as though for approval, "I am going to the doctor tomorrow because I feel like I have a sinus infection . So I'll miss a few hours of work."

"What are you apologizing for?" Tom asked, trying to lighten the mood. "Your health comes first."

Lance nodded but still fidgeted nervously. Finally, he said: "I'm sorry, Tom. I think I just threw up on you."

"What?"

"I feel like I just threw up everything on you…because…well, we don't get to talk very much, and you caught me off guard by coming into my office."

Tom shook his head. "You have nothing to apologize for. It's great to hear how you are doing. I just want you to know that I appreciate you, Lance. And I love that we get to do this together."

"Me too," said Lance, looking relieved.

"See you on Sunday," Tom said with a goodbye wave.

As Tom left, something about the conversation troubled him. Lance had seemed so surprised to see him and then so quick to apologize for telling Tom about his life. Had Tom really become so isolated and grouchy over the years?

Tom made his way to his youth and childrens' pastor's office. "Hello," he rapped on the

door. "Is anyone here?"

Silence.

Tom moved on to his discipleship and groups pastor, James, only to find that his lights were out and the door closed and locked.

Tom looked at his phone and saw that it was only 10:30am on Thursday morning. And no one but his needy and quite possibly sick worship leader and his assistant Margaret were in the building.

Tom knew what he had to do, but he hated to do it.

Tom had friends who ran much larger organizations where every team member reported to Human Resources. If they wanted a half day off, they reported that half day to HR. If they wanted to take a week's vacation at Thanksgiving, they put in for that time off with the HR office. If they wanted to buy something for their work, they checked out a credit card from HR. And when they got into the office, went to lunch, and left for the day they moved their little dots on the white board to show where they were.

It was painful to even think about this kind of culture. What had happened to the days when his employees had been invested 110% because they loved their work?

And how wrapped up had he been in his own world that he hadn't noticed the change until now?

Tom knew his team needed to take their jobs more seriously, and being in the office 9-5 was part of that. No wonder he was so stressed all the time, if no one else was doing their work!

Next week, Tom would teach them a lesson. He sent an email to Margaret.

"Margaret, please pick me up one large white board and eleven different colored small circular magnets. I am going to create a board to put in your office where our team will begin to check in and out of the office each day."

Pressing send, Tom put away that project and returned to the weekend message preparation.

Thursday afternoon was Tom's time to preach the message out loud to an empty auditorium. This was a discipline that had been started years earlier, just after a conference, when Tom heard a well-respected leader talk about his rehearsal routine and state that he never stepped on stage without having spoken his message at least six times to an empty room. That seemed like a great way to excel, so Tom did it.

This task had started to feel arduous in recent years, and Tom often found that he was bored with the message long before he ever delivered it. But the discipline yielded great results; Tom had the message so dialed in by Sunday that he made public speaking look easy.

So he took to the empty stage and began to deliver his message.

As he began to talk he felt confident, and the worries of the day began to melt away. With the thought of living in grace on his mind, he was able to let go of everything else happening in his office and in his life.

He felt light. He felt free.

This, Tom thought, *is how things should be.*

Now how do I keep it this way?

Chapter 22

Several times throughout the Sunday services, Tom felt anxiety rise in his chest while he was teaching; he locked eyes with people in the crowd who he had said 'no' to in the past few days.

As he spoke to the crowd the courtroom in his mind was in session once again.

I should have taken him up on his offer for coffee.

I should have said yes to going to his 50th birthday party.

We should invite them over for dinner next week, since I said no this week.

But as each should arose, Tom let it go in grace. Those things were not the most important things in his life. They could wait. And if they never came to pass, it wouldn't affect April or Thomas. It wouldn't be the end of the world.

Sunday came and went without a hitch except for the anxiety rising in Tom's chest. Tom was off to the cabin by 5:00pm.

The pine needles, twigs, and logs were all gathered in order. The IPA was cracked open and the Dallas Cowboys were on Sunday Night Football. Tom loved SNF, and he hated the Cowboys - a killer combination for this Sunday evening.

Monday morning came, and Tom picked up the cabin's landline to call Hank. Two rings and Hank picked up, cheerful as ever.

But without even saying 'hello,' Tom said: "Well, it has been a helluva week."

Tom didn't usually swear, but this was a half swear, and he felt freer with Hank than he did when speaking to anyone else.

"Tell me about it," Hank requested.

"In short:

"My team is lazy.

"My wife and I are living incongruent lives.

"I missed my son's academic awards ceremony. April never reminded me!

"So it's no wonder I feel so overwhelmed all the time!

"I am working my ass off," Tom swore, officially this time,

"and it seems like everyone around me is happy to just coast. No wonder I'm so stressed if I'm always picking up the pieces."

When Tom was done talking, Hank didn't answer immediately. He paused for a moment of contemplation. "It sounds like you have a gap," he pronounced, finally. "A gap between how you think others should act, and how they do. And it sounds like you have spent a good part of this week shoulding on others."

Tom bristled. "Some shoulds *are* true. My team should do the work I pay them to do!"

"Tom," Hank asked, "do you still have the journal from last week?"

"Of course."

"I want you to write down these words:

I should on others when I …

"Shoot," said Tom, barely bypassing cussing for a third time in less than two minutes.

"I do should on others. A lot. But what else am I supposed to do?"

"Let me ask you something, Tom. Do you have job descriptions for all your team at church?"

"Yes, of course," said Tom.

"And I'll bet ," Hank continued, "that whether you realize it or not, you have a job description for pretty much every person in your life! You have pretty specific expectations of what people need to do for you."

"For April, for instance: 'When I'm talking I need you to listen, and when you're talking I need to be doing other things, but I'll nod my head like I'm listening!'

"For your friends: 'You should always offer to drive me to the airport, and you should never ask me to drive you to the airport.'

"For your mom: 'Let me live my life.'

"For your son Thomas, 'Let me live your life.'

"Tom, I'm half-joking about all of this, but I think you have a problem shoulding all over others," Hank said.

Tom thought about this. The way Hank had described his thinking wasn't very flattering.

"You have a list of things your team should and should not do. You have become very skilled at having a set of expectations for your team that exists outside of their agreed-upon job descriptions. Tell me, Tom, is your team getting their jobs done?"

"I guess they must be," Tom admitted. "I would have noticed earlier if they weren't." He still felt a pang of guilt at how long it had taken him to realize how empty the church offices were during work hours.

"Right. So whatever they're doing, it's working to fulfill the job descriptions you have set up for them.

"Yet you make your team feel guilty when they don't meet your expectations. When they don't meet your expectations, you can get frustrated, stressed out, or start to suspect that they are lazy, uncommitted, or unqualified. Even though the assigned work is getting done. If they don't appear to be working *hard enough*, that's a problem for you.

"Is any of this making sense?" asked Hank.

Tom was silent.

Hank continued.

"In the gospel of Matthew…

"Jesus says… "Do not judge, or you too will be judged.
For in the same way you judge others, you will be judged,
and with the measure you use, it will be measured to you.
Why do you look at the speck of sawdust in your brother's
eye and pay no attention to the plank in your own eye?
How can you say to your brother, 'Let me take the speck
out of your eye,' when all the time there is a plank in your
own eye? You hypocrite, first take the plank out of your
own eye, and then you will see clearly to remove the speck
from your brother's eye."

"Be careful about shoulding on others, Tom. Because if you should on others, you're gonna get a lot of should on yourself."

Hank chuckled. "I know that's a paraphrase, but that's pretty much what Jesus said!

"The shoulds are like a boomerang, Tom. The more you should on others, the more they will should on you."

"Well it's not like I started it!" Tom said defensively, though he hated how childish he sounded, even to himself. "You don't think my team shoulds on me?"

"Of course they do, Tom," Hank agreed. "But that's next week's topic!

"For now, let's stay on topic and how you have private plans for your team, your wife, your son and pretty much everyone you meet.

"Let's break this down, Tom:

You have expectations of other people.

These people are completely unaware of your expectations for them.

They quickly fail to meet your secret expectations.

You get angry with them and should all over them.

"That is the simple succession of shoulding on others."

Tom was silent for a moment, thinking about that.

"Remember the famous verse in Jeremiah 29:11, Tom?" Hank asked.

"'For I know the plans I have for you,' declares the Lord, 'plans to prosper you and not to harm you, plans to give you hope and a future.'"

"When we should on others, we have plans for people's lives. But we aren't God, so we're not very good at it.

"'For I know the plans I have for you,' declares Tom, 'plans to prosper me and not to harm me, plans to do what I want now, and in the future.'"

"Ouch," Tom winced, realizing he had played the role of God in so many people's lives. He had created private job descriptions for people that were largely meant to serve him and further his agenda.

How selfish.

How hurtful.

Who was he, to think that he was God?

Hank couldn't see it over the phone, but Tom's head was in his hands. His eyes were stinging with tears again. "Can we be done for today?" Tom asked. "I have a lot to pray about and ask God's forgiveness for today."

"Sure," said Hank, his voice warm and comforting. "But can I pray for you before I let you go?"

"Please," said Tom.

"Dear perfect God,

"Please have mercy on our less than perfect lives.

"Please remind us of your plan and let our plans dissolve.

"Please be with Tom as he seeks you today.

"Allow his mind to be clear and his heart to be resolved to serve you and bless others.

"Let Tom step out of this unwinnable race and rest in your grace."

"Amen."

After a long pause, Tom hung up the phone.

He wondered what the next week would bring.

Chapter 23

Tom returned home with new eyes. He had begun to free himself of shoulds, but hadn't managed to free others from his own.

He quickly realized how deeply he'd buried his wife, son, staff and others under his secret burdens.

He'd basically should all over everyone.

It always started with the "price tag" idea. Is this person measuring up? Are they behaving in a worthy way?

That quickly evolved into being judgmental, imposing his plans and ideas on others' lives, and holding people accountable to secret job descriptions he had written for them. All without any right to do so. All without anyone's knowledge.

Tom had a very sober week. He felt guilty because there were so many good shoulds that he would never get to. The habit of shoulding, he realized, would take time to break.

By Tuesday afternoon, Tom felt out of gas. If you could see the fuel level of his heart, it was below empty.

Being hard on himself and simultaneously trying to spend the week serving and living up to the expectations of others was mentally, physically, emotionally, relationally and spiritually exhausting.

Tom kept praying for God to fill him up, but it felt like he leaked fuel quicker than God could fill. Or quicker than God chose to fill.

Maybe He is trying to teach me a lesson, Tom thought.

By the time Sunday arrived Tom had served people all week, trying to be full of energy and extend compassion to everyone he met. Then speaking to the congregation on Sunday, three times, back to back to back...his fuel level was far below "E," and he hadn't even known that was possible.

Isn't empty really empty? he thought.

I wonder how long I can run on empty.

It seemed like he would have no choice but to try.

April and Thomas had a birthday party right after church, which allowed Tom to head to the cabin as soon as the last service ended.

As the service host was finishing up offerings and announcements, Tom was already in his car on the way to the mountains.

By the time the band had sung the final song and the third service ended, Tom was already twenty-two minutes down the road. He had his overnight bag in the car with his backpack and computer.

He would wear the same clothes the next few days in the mountains.

That will at least save effort and energy, he thought.

And he wondered how much longer he could keep doing this.

✱✱✱

As April sat at the birthday party, she thought about her Tom. She was impressed by how Tom was changing.

He still screwed up at times. He still forgot events and glazed over a little when she was talking to him.

But sometimes, he didn't. Sometimes she expected him to tense in anger when something went wrong, and he relaxed and smiled instead.

Sometimes she finished a project and stepped out of her office to find Tom doing dishes or starting dinner. At those times he'd smile at her, almost sheepishly. Almost shyly. Like he had so many years ago.

Sometimes she came home from her errands to hear him talking to Thomas quietly in the next room.

She still worried about Tom. He still seemed to be on the trajectory he'd had for years: one of growing more and more burdened, more and more tired, more and more absent from daily life. It was like he was more comfortable and accustomed to living in the future, than being present in the now.

But sometimes, he'd come back.

April hoped that he would live in the present more often.

✱✱✱

Tom had known that something had to change for a long time. At first Hank's teachings had given him hope. But now he wondered what was missing. Why did he still feel so incomplete even though he'd done his best to stop shoulding on himself and others?

What part of grace was he missing?

Just seventy minutes removed from the stage, Tom was pulling his car up to the edge of the long walkway that led to the door of his nearby, faraway place.

Tom stood and looked down the old wood planks. This was the place where he came to recharge. This was the place where he came when he was running on empty.

Good and bad, happy and sad are waiting inside, he thought to himself.

Through the years, his mountain retreat had bookended the best and worst of times for Tom.

There were family vacations, retreats with his kids, birthday celebrations and Thanksgiving.

There were thin space moments where it seemed God was close enough to touch.

There were days of uninvited silence where God refused to speak. Moments he felt like throwing in the towel on everything short of living.

Tonight, he sensed, would be one of those nights.

When Tom felt empty, sin was close. It was like an old habit that knew precisely when to knock.

It was hard to say 'no' to this when he felt like all he had said was 'yes' to everyone all week.

Settling into a familiar place on the couch, Tom quickly downed a first then grabbed his second IPA microbrew. Tom knew where this led, but he felt too drained to stop himself.

Surfing social media was usually harmless, but not when Tom was on empty. When he was on empty, things that would never have tempted him on full became hard to resist. Pictures he would have scrolled past without a second thought became pictures he clicked on, finding more and more similar and more risque images.

Tom remembered a simple outline he had written on an American Airlines napkin several years back. He had preached this to hundreds of people, but had not admitted how personal it was to him.

Tom could hear himself saying to others, "When surfing Twitter, Instagram or Facebook we are going to stumble onto tempting material. It's not if, it's when.

"When that happens, do we confess it and draw strength from our friends, setting up guardrails if necessary?

"Or do we cover it up and hide in shame until we find ourselves seeking it out again?

"If we hide ourselves in shame, it becomes easier to fall prey to this temptation again. One of the devil's most powerful lies is, 'you are not good enough.' When we allow ourselves to feel defeated by this temptation, we fall prey to it again and again.

"So what can we do when temptation comes knocking? We can be honest with ourselves. We can draw strength from others."

Had Tom done this himself? No. It was too hard for him to admit that a successful leader could be tempted. It almost felt frightening. What would people think if they knew he had these thoughts?

And yet, most people had them. He knew they did. This was what he told his congregants year after year. He urged them to be honest and draw strength from each other.

But Tom rarely did.

Preaching is so much easier than life, thought Tom.

Now with more guilt, Tom threw in the towel and went to bed.

It was clear that he'd reached his limit.

What else could possibly happen.

Chapter 24

The Monday morning call with Hank was not welcome. In fact, Tom dreaded it.

Tom knew he *should* be eager to talk to Hank, but he felt ashamed of where he was today. He figured that somehow Hank would be able to see through the phone and chide Tom about everything he had done or failed to do this week.

Still, he picked up the phone, braced himself, and pressed the call button.

"Hello Tom," Hank said warmly after three rings. "How was your week?"

"I am tired," said Tom. He knew his tone of voice said more than the words.

Hank said nothing. Paused, waiting. Listening.

Tom sighed. "I feel like all my serving others and trying to love everyone has led me to the edge of a very slippery slope. I find it so easy to fall into sin when I'm on empty. And somehow, here I am again despite our talks. I felt so good after the last time I talked to you, Hank. But now I feel like I'm just right back where I was before."

Tom swore he could *hear* Hank's understanding nod through the phone. "Let me ask you a question, Tom. What have you said yes to this week? I mean, literally. Everything. Could you share with me everything and everyone you have said 'yes' to this past week?"

Tom began the list:

• My wife who wanted me to get up early for a walk Tuesday morning
• My assistant who wanted to know if I could get her the weekend message outline on Tuesday by noon instead of 5:00pm because she had a doctor's appointment
• My youth pastor needed time off because his wife is feeling fat after the baby.
• One of my board members is about to go through a

divorce, which will likely cause him to step off our board, so we had a late dinner, after my dinner at home with April and Thomas, Tuesday night.

• Wednesday morning, I said 'yes' to a breakfast with an old friend who is in town. That made me late to our staff meeting where I had agreed two weeks ago to roll out ideas for this coming year.

Tom went on for another five minutes before Hank stopped him.

"That's enough, Tom. We are only half way through the week, and you have poured yourself out to at least twenty-five people.

"Let me ask you another question, Tom. What have you said 'no' to this week?"

Tom took nearly two minutes of silence to think of something he'd said 'no' to, but then he proudly announced: "I told a church in Texas that I could not come to speak this summer at their men's conference!"

"That's great, Tom!" said Hank. "And what else?"

As Tom thought, he felt like there was not enough fuel in his mental tank to take him where Hank wanted him to go.

"I'm tired, Hank. I don't know what to say. I am sure I have said 'no' to other things this week, but…"

Hank interrupted, "Have you ever gotten so busy driving your car that you nearly ran out of gas? Have you ever looked at the gas gauge on your car and seen it register 'E' or even below 'E?'

"I have to admit something to you, Tom, that most people hate to admit. I have run my car out of gas at least three times in the past two years!

"I get going from meeting to meeting and forget to even look at the gauge that is fifteen inches in front of me! As the gauge moves closer to 'E' and there's no gas station in sight…I start to pray. And there is something inside me that believes I can actually keep driving the car on willpower alone.

"'I have faith that I will have enough gas to get to this last meeting. If God just helps me make it that far, *then* I will get more gas!'

"Bottom line, I have run out of gas multiple times and missed several meetings. And I've been asking God to do things He should never have had to do because I refused to recognize my limitations and stay inside of them.

"Tom, hold on for a quick turn here. You are out of gas, my friend.

"I want you to take a moment to imagine that you are driving through life. You've been driving and driving and driving, your eyes always on the stretch of road ahead. Now would you take your eyes off the road for a second and put them on the gas gauge?

"Let's say this gas gauge could register what's in your heart. What is it reading right now? Is it on F for full? Or on E for empty? Maybe you have half a tank, but it's falling fast?"

"I'm below the E," Tom said bluntly. It felt good to finally admit that to someone, but that didn't change the empty feeling.

"I agree," Hank said. "You are running on empty. But do you know why you feel so out of gas?" Hank didn't wait for Tom's answer. "You are letting others should all over you, Tom!

"The private pressures from the shoulds of others can be more intrusive and even heavier than the shoulds we heap upon ourselves. Their private ideas about what we should do and our agreement, that yes, we *should* do them, can be even heavier than our own ideas about what we should do."

"Yes," said Tom, feeling vindicated. "The shoulds of others make me feel so defensive and angry! It's like other people are trying to enforce what they want for my life. But it's *my* life.

"I know it's my life. Yet it still feels like I have all these people judging and evaluating me all the time." Tom felt so frustrated as he said that, but he didn't know what to do.

"Have you ever watched Olympic figure skating?" Hank asked, out of nowhere. Tom was silent, unsure what to say to the sudden change in topic.

"In Olympic figure skating," Hank continued, "the judges choose certain things that the skaters need to do. A toe loop, a double axel, a triple salchow, whatever that means. And the skaters have to do it, and the judges rank them on how well they perform each move.

"In all my years of listening to leaders, I have seen this type of system play out in life as well.

"You've got your mother, who demanded straight A's. When you came home with your report card, she'd hold up her judge's card of approval or disapproval.

"Maybe your father wanted you to be a star and excel in sports just like he did when he was younger. He was at every game, watching, judging, scoring your progress and performance. Giving you his approval or disapproval.

"Maybe you had a grandparent who had your career all planned out for you, since you were born. Never mind that it may not be what you wanted to do. They always approved or disapproved of everything you did, based on whether it fit *their* plan for your life.

"You might have had a boss who thought you should stay late on weekdays or come in to work on Saturdays, even though your job description said forty hours. When you left to go home, it's like you could see him standing in the judge's box, holding up a scorecard, and it wasn't good.

"Or maybe you have a friend who has the expectation that you should always be available to hang out and instantly respond to every text. You enjoy your friend, but his neediness is draining.

"It takes your tank to empty and then even lower. Eventually, you run out of gas, and in an attempt to do everything, you find yourself feeling numb and empty and not able to do anything."

"That's exactly how I feel! But how do I stop others from shoulding all over me?" Tom asked, irritated. "It's not like I can magically change their behavior."

"That's absolutely right, Tom. You can't. You can't control *anyone's* behavior but your own. But what you can do is refuse to be bothered by their judgements. You can stop saying 'yes.'

"Part of you will feel like that's wrong, as though you *should* live up to these people's expectations. As though you are *causing* them distress if you don't. But *you* aren't causing anything. They are causing their own distress by having these expectations you didn't invite or ask for.

"You can't stop people from doing that. But you can't live up to all their expectations and still have fuel to do what you should, either. You can only control one person's gas tank: your own.

"There is one way you can *encourage* them to keep shoulding on you, and that's to keep saying 'yes.' As you keep saying 'yes,' you teach people that their expectations of you are correct and *should* be met. And the burden gets heavier and heavier.

"When you say 'yes' to their shoulds, others will should on you even more and get even more upset when you don't meet their expectations. You will start to get angry at others and even bitter as you feel like you are no longer doing what you want to do, what you should do, or what God has called you to do!

"You will eventually start to feel like your life is not your own as you keep saying 'yes' to the life others feel you should live.

"What I have learned through many years of counseling leaders and leading my own life is this:

"When I'm obsessed with your yes, my life becomes a mess.

"When I live my life according to what other people want, I'm not living my life. I'm living someone else's version of my life. It's not what I want. It's not what God wants. It's not what He created me for. It's what other humans want for me. When I'm obsessed with your yes, my life becomes a mess.

"But there's an easy way to escape this cycle, Tom.

"When I'm obsessed with God's yes, my life becomes blessed.

"When I stop worrying about what you want and what you think, and instead I focus on what God wants and what God thinks, then:

- I start to live out my unique design.
- I feel free and empowered instead of burdened.
- I'm living according to the plan of someone who knows and loves me even better than I know and love myself.

The problem is that we feel like we have to always say 'yes' to the expectations and demands of others, but we don't.

"Even when those demands follow good shoulds, as we've seen, there are far too many of those for anyone to ever complete them all. God made many people, with many different talents, because it takes many different people to fulfil all the good shoulds.

Even if another person has expectations of you that seem good to them, they may not be the same expectations God made you to fulfill.

"So if you listen to that person's shoulds, even good shoulds, the work God has for you may go undone. And you won't feel filled up and full of purpose if you aren't doing what God made you for.

"We can humbly but confidently say 'no' to the expectations and demands of others.

"Remember the notion of not allowing the devil to become your mentor, Tom? This lesson is about that, too. When we act out of *fear* of rejection or letting someone down, we are not acting out of *love*. There is nothing technically *wrong* with what we're doing, except that we're ignoring the love God put in our hearts, and we may end up running way below empty. We may end up with nothing left in our tank to do the work God has for us or to resist sin.

"And that's how the devil gets you, using fear instead of love. We have to stop being afraid of rejection and of disappointing others if we want to walk the path God truly has for us.

"Even righteous people can sometimes get mixed up and think *they* know what God wants for another person. Look at how you have should on the people in your life, Tom! It's no surprise that they would do the same to you, and it isn't any better.

"We find a hidden truth for our lives in plain sight as we look at a side of Jesus that no one wants to study. Let's look at all the times that Jesus said 'no.'"

Tom found it hard to imagine Jesus - the perfect, and the infinite - saying 'no' to a righteous request. But Hank said the Bible included many examples of this.

Was Tom shoulding so hard he projected his shoulds onto Jesus, too?

Chapter 25

"Jesus was compassionate, and Jesus was a servant," Hank explained patiently. "So He often said 'yes' to those who had true faith or were truly in need. He said 'yes' when it was the right thing to do, when it was a key part of his mission.

"But when the request was wrong, when people made demands or tried to enforce their priorities and timing on Him, Jesus said 'no.'

"He said 'no' pretty emphatically when people tried to turn others' acts of worship into profit for themselves. When people asked Him to follow the old law, with a spirit of love enforcing His priorities, Jesus said 'no.'

"Jesus was very comfortable saying 'no.'" For instance, Jesus said 'no' to His friends. Take a look at this, Tom:

"Mark 10:35-37, Then James and John, the sons of Zebedee, came to him. "Teacher," they said, "we want you to do for us whatever we ask." "What do you want me to do for you?" He asked. "They replied, "Let one of us sit at your right and the other at your left in your glory."

"Their request was: 'When you come into power, we want to be your second and third in command. We want to be the most powerful, other than you, of course, Jesus!'

"Tom, have you ever had a friend try to use their personal relationship with you to get something they wouldn't be able to get without you?

"Have you ever had a close friend ask you for something that you knew you should say, 'no' to, but it was your friend, so you felt like you couldn't say 'no?'

"Mark 10:38-40, "You don't know what you are asking," Jesus said. "Can you drink the cup I drink or be baptized with the baptism I am baptized with?"

"We can," they answered. Jesus said to them,
"You will drink the cup I drink and be baptized with
the baptism I am baptized with, but to sit at my
right or left is not for me to grant. These places belong
to those for whom they have been prepared."

They were His friends, but Jesus said 'no.'

Jesus also said 'no' to positive peer pressure and promotions. He said 'no' to good publicity when He knew it would damage His mission:

"John 6:14-15, "When the people saw Him do this
miraculous sign, they exclaimed, 'Surely, He is the Prophet
we have been expecting!' When Jesus saw that they were
ready to force Him to be their king, He slipped away
into the hills by Himself."

"Tom, have you ever had people offer you something that you knew wasn't right for you, but it was something really cool? You know you should say 'no' but it would be so easy to say 'yes,' and everyone wants you to say 'yes.'

"These people want to make Jesus their king. But Jesus didn't come to earth to be a king. He was a king before He came to earth. He came to earth to be a crucified Savior.

"Jesus didn't say, 'Well, if you insist,' or, 'Let me think about it, maybe I should be a king.'

"He just said 'no' to really cool positive peer pressure and pro-motions that would make Him more popular. Someone could even have argued that becoming king would have helped Him save more souls, but Jesus knew God's plan was different. So He said 'no.'

"Jesus also said 'no' to solving everyone's problems:

"Luke 12:13, "Then someone called from the crowd,
'Teacher, please tell my brother to divide our father's
estate with me.'"

"Tom, I know your days and weeks are full of people bringing their problems to you. They have nothing to do with you, but they bring them to you and complain to you. They may ask you to take sides, or to resolve an issue that's not your issue. And when people ask for your help like that, it feels like you have to say 'yes.'

"That's what this guy does with Jesus. He asks Jesus to intervene in his situation. And it seems like a reasonable request. Sharing the family inheritance is the right thing to do. This is an easy yes, right?

"Luke 12:14-15, "Jesus replied, 'Friend, who made me a judge over you to decide such things as that?' Then He said, 'Beware! Guard against every kind of greed. Life is not measured by how much you own.'"

"It's an easy 'yes,' but Jesus says 'no.' Why? Well, He says it's not His purpose to judge such things.

"Jesus didn't feel obliged to solve everyone's problems.

"Jesus didn't feel obliged to always give people what they wanted.

"Jesus knew that sometimes 'no' is the best answer for people, so they can use their minds and work out their own problems. Or because His time and energy must be reserved for elsewhere.

"Jesus also said 'no' to helping everyone all the time:

"Mark 1:29-31, "After Jesus left the synagogue with James and John, they went to Simon and Andrew's home. Now Simon's mother-in-law was sick in bed with a high fever. They told Jesus about her right away. So, He went to her bedside, took her by the hand, and helped her sit up. Then the fever left her, and she prepared a meal for them."

"Some people consider this the greatest miracle in the entire Bible. Jesus heals Peter's mother-in-law! Would you want Jesus to heal your mother-in-law?" chuckled Hank. "Don't answer that.

"Jesus heals Peter's mother-in-law, and word gets out about it."

"Mark 1:32-37, That evening after sunset,
many sick and demon-possessed people were brought to
Jesus. The whole town gathered at the door to watch.
So, Jesus healed many people who were sick with
various diseases, and He cast out many demons.
But because the demons knew who He was, He did
not allow them to speak. Before daybreak the next
morning, Jesus got up and went out to an isolated place
to pray. Later Simon and the others went out to find Him.
When they found Him, they said, "Everyone is looking for you."

"Tom, there is no doubt that a big part of your job is helping people. And we are all called to help others.

"We should help others.

"This is a good should!

"But maybe you've been helping people a lot. Maybe you haven't had any time to take care of yourself. Maybe you haven't had any time to be with God. Maybe now you're afraid you don't have anything left to perform an even greater good, or you're afraid that people are coming to depend on you too much instead of solving their own problems.

"But the people who are asking for help are asking for something good. They're asking for help, so you have to say 'yes,' right?

"Jesus didn't.

"He healed people, but then He needed some time alone.

"You can hear it in the voice of Simon: 'Everyone's looking for you. What are you doing? You should be healing people and not just off by yourself!'

"But Jesus was by Himself. He was alone, so He could pray.

"It's kind of mind-boggling; Jesus was the most compassionate person to ever walk on this planet. He came to save people, including these people. His desire was for them to put their faith in Him, so you'd think He'd say 'yes' to all of their demands and requests and certainly to them asking Him for help. But sometimes Jesus said, 'no.' Why did He say 'no?'

"Remember what we talked about several weeks ago, Tom? The fact that even Jesus did not have an unlimited capacity to care?

"Jesus knew He had to steward His compassion.

"You know what I mean by 'steward,' right? To steward something is to oversee the administration of it. To help budget and allocate the distribution of a resource. Basically, it's to make good use of that resource. It's to use it wisely so that it grows and becomes greater, instead of using it carelessly so that it gets all used up and there isn't any more when you need it."

Tom thought about that.

"For instance, we have to steward our money and our time, right? Because we realize we only have a certain amount of money and time. We don't have an inexhaustible supply. We can't just keep spending it, or we'll run out. So we have to be careful with how we spend it, especially if we want to have more of it to use for good causes over the years.

"Tom, this is one of the truest and strangest things I have learned over the years as I have spent time leading leaders:

"We may not realize it, but this is also true of our compassion. At any one time, we only have a certain amount. We don't have an inexhaustible amount, so if we give away too much, we'll end up - well, exhausted.

"So we must steward our compassion.

"As humans, we're limited.

"God is not limited. But when Jesus, who is God, decided to live a human life, He chose to limit Himself. In just the same way that He rested on the seventh day in Genesis. God certainly didn't *need* to rest; He could have kept right on going. But He knew that we would need this example because He did not make *us* to be unlimited. He made us limited, so we would have to work together.

"What's interesting to me is that Jesus accepted those limitations in such an easy way. He wasn't able to do everything that everyone wanted Him to, but we get no sense that He felt guilty about that. We have no sense that He resented his limitations.

"Jesus couldn't always prioritize serving people; He often

prioritized time with God over serving people, but He knew that was the right thing to do. He knew it was what he needed to do.

"He wasn't defensive.

"He didn't overextend Himself.

"He said 'no.'

"He took naps!

"Tom, I know you are the communicator between the two of us, but here are several things I have learned from Jesus that fit this season of your life:

"Saying 'no' is not necessarily un-Christlike, but it can be just a humble admission of your limitations.

"It's not always right to alleviate every burden of others. Sometimes it may be more loving to allow people to carry that burden, so they can experience the necessary growth they need or learn the necessary consequences of their decisions.

"And, probably more than anything else, we learn from Jesus that sometimes it's more important to go up on the mountain and be filled by God than to stay down in the valley and pour yourself out for others.

"Like Jesus, we can say 'no.'

"Does this make sense?" asked Hank.

"It does," said Tom soberly. "I need to be careful about saying 'yes' to every good thing, so I can have energy on reserve to say 'yes' to the best things."

"I think we are getting somewhere," Hank pronounced.

"Yes. This wisdom is filling my tank," said Tom. They both agreed to talk again in a week.

Tom remembered how he'd felt when he first started letting go of his shoulds.

He wondered if he could feel that way again.

Chapter 26

The time with Hank was moving. The man's reputation for changing lives was well-deserved.

Tom felt the understandings inside himself begin to change. He knew he had to write what he was feeling as soon as he hung up the phone. He pulled out his computer and examined the feelings Hank had left him with.

It had been a long time since Tom had written anything that wasn't due that week. As he looked at the blinking cursor on his computer screen, he began to line up pixels into words.

How do we prevent others from shoulding on us? Tom wondered.

What are the critical questions a person must answer in order to be able to say 'no' with humility, grace and confidence?

"First," he found himself typing, "you must know who you are. When we say 'yes' to everything that's asked of us, we are allowing our identity to be determined by others, and it rarely works. It rarely feels comfortable.

"If I say 'yes' to everything you think I should be, I am letting you determine my identity. That's not your job. It's God's.

"I can say 'no' to the shoulds of others because of what God says about me," he wrote.

Then Tom was hit by a sudden bolt of inspiration: "When Jesus was baptised, God spoke from Heaven: 'You are my Son whom I love; with you I am well pleased.' That's why Jesus was able to say 'no.' He knew who He was: God's son, loved perfectly by Him.

"That's who I am.

"That's who you are.

"We are God's children.

"We are loved perfectly by Him.

"Knowing who we are helps us to say 'no.'

"It keeps our vision vertical instead of horizontal."

Tom continued writing: "We should on others and let others

should on us when we forget who our audience is.

We think it's other people with human values. We think we have to please them or that *they* have to please *us*."

"Our audience isn't other people. It's God."

1 Thessalonians 2:4, "Our purpose is to please
God, not people. He alone examines the motives of our hearts."

"We need to keep our vision vertical. We live to please God. If He is well pleased, that is what ultimately matters. That allows us to say 'no.'

"It allows us to shed the shoulds!"

Tom remembered Hank's perfectly-constructed words:

"When I'm obsessed with your yes,
"my life becomes a mess.
"When I'm obsessed with God's yes,
"my life becomes blessed."

Jesus could say 'no' with humility, grace and confidence because He knew who He was. He knew His audience and was filled with God's love.

Jesus was never on empty because He prioritized His time with God.

At that moment, Tom knew what he must do.

He closed the computer and got down on his knees.

"God, please help me keep my eyes on you.

"Forgive me for the times I have allowed others to dictate who I am. God, please cause me to want to want you more and to value my time with you more.

"Allow me to realize that taking care of myself isn't selfish. It is necessary to increase my ability to do Your work.

"Spirit, fill me up so I can pour myself out.

"Teach me to fill myself, so I always have enough to give.

"Fill me up so I can say 'yes' and do the things I should do to serve others and grow your Kingdom forward. Amen."

Tom stood up feeling like a new man. He felt free.

He sent a text message to Hank, thanking him for the past three weeks which had completely refreshed and refocused his life, family and ministry.

It was an hour later when Hank replied:

"One last thing, Tom. There is a final should that we need to address next Monday."

Tom texted that next Monday would be difficult.

"I really feel like my life is on track now."

Hank urged Tom to call and explained that next week's call would address the final and most critical should of all.

Tom hoped that after letting go of that should, he could be truly free.

Chapter 27

When Tom came home smiling, April felt like the sun was rising again. When he swept her up in his arms in the driveway and spun her around just like old times, she clung to him and squealed.

That glow stayed with her as she followed him into the house, as he bounded up to Thomas and asked how his day had been. It stayed with her as Thomas babbled excitedly, recounting every detail of what he'd done at school.

April felt like she was floating as she drifted into the kitchen to start dinner. As she did, she noticed that Tom had washed his coffee cup and placed it in the drain basket.

It felt like Tom was finally *here* again.

April had to find out what he was doing. And maybe she needed to try it, too.

✱✱✱

The next week was hectic. Tom let go of his shoulds as best he could and found himself being a better servant to himself and others.

But there was still a simmering discontentment underneath it all, underneath his own limitations.

Why couldn't he have an infinite gas tank like he wanted?

Why couldn't things be easier?

Monday morning arrived, and Tom was not able to make it back to the mountains. There was so much going on with Christmas quickly approaching, and Tom was needed at home. He felt full enough, after a week of practicing saying 'no,' to skip his weekly cabin retreat.

So instead of his cabin in the mountains, he called Hank from his office at church.

Hank picked up quickly, as always. Tom explained he was calling from his office, and he didn't have a lot of time.

"Thanks for calling, Tom," Hank said immediately. "Your office is the perfect environment for today's conversation."

Tom felt himself frowning, looking around, and wondering, *why?*

Hank answered his question before he could ask it. "Tom, look around your office," Hank instructed. "Do you have Bibles in your office? Are there any photos of Israel? What about crosses? Are there any crosses in your office, Tom?"

"Four or five of them," Tom answered, casting his eyes about the room. There were crosses on the Bibles themselves, wooden crosses on the walls. There were crosses on the printed certificates that hung on his walls.

"We have talked about shoulding on yourself and others," Hank continued. "Who is left, Tom? Who have you dedicated your life to proclaiming and following?"

Myself. Others. Who else? Tom thought he was home free when one final, terrifying thought crossed his mind.

I should on God when...

Tom could barely speak the sentence.

"I should on God," Tom said quietly.

"Yes, you do," said Hank matter-of-factly. "And you are not alone in this. Every human who has walked this planet has done their fair share of shoulding on God, just like they should on themselves and others.

"In fact, consider your neighborhood, Tom. All those people who live in front of you, behind you and beside you...do they all go to church? Are they all involved in some kind of faith community?"

"No," said Tom. "Most of them spend Saturday afternoon washing the car or Sunday morning messing around with the water sprinklers in their yard."

"Exactly. And why don't your neighbors, or for that matter, other people in your city or state, go to church or even consider joining a faith community?"

In typical Hank style, he didn't wait for a reply.

"It's probably because at some point, they should on God."

"When they were in the 4th grade, their mom got sick. They were part of a church and most of what they remember is everyone was praying for their mom to get better. They even remember people coming to the house to bring food and pray over their mom and family. It seemed like the whole world was probably praying!

"And yet it seemed like God wasn't listening. Mom got sicker. And when they were entering into 5th grade, Mom passed away. Everyone was praying, and God should have healed their mom. And from the 5th grade forward, God got should on.

"Or maybe at some point they had a bad experience with a church. Maybe they had a pastor who should all over *them* and passed judgement on them when they didn't do what he wanted. Maybe they even had a pastor who failed the congregation in some way, and now they think that's what God is like.

"That neighbor who lives in front of you, behind you and beside you … they should on God. He should have made their pastor behave better.

"Maybe it's a couple in their late thirties who know they need to make an effort to get their family and their child to church. They rearrange life so that church fits. They make sure their child is at youth group every week and camp every summer. Much of their life revolves around church during the teenage years as it seems like this is the formula for God's blessing and protection.

"But at some point, their child has a bad experience. They decide this church thing might not be for them. So as their child's car is pulling out of the driveway for college, they are also pulling away from their faith. No more church for years to come, after all that church for so many years!

"And that couple who lives in your city…they should on God. 'We held up our end of the bargain. We sacrificed and got our child to church every week! God, you owe us a son or daughter that lives and walks in faith. We know what God's will should be for our son or daughter, and they're not doing it!'

"You see, Tom, every single person who has walked this planet has moments in life where God…"

"…did not act like He should," Tom finished.

"Exactly," Hank agreed.

"And when that happens," Tom ventured, "people should on God."

"We should on God because we make private pacts and contracts that we believe He should keep.

"Everyone prayed…there was a pact…He should heal my mom. Why bother praying if God isn't going to do what I want?

"We got our son or daughter to youth group every week…there is a contract. He should have kept our child close and on fire in their faith. Why bother going to church if our kids will just leave it?

"We should on God when He does not act like we think He should.

"The problem is, God hardly ever acts like we think He should. And we certainly do not make pacts and private contracts with God that He is liable to uphold. God's ways are not our ways, and His foolishness is wiser than our wisdom."

Tom recognized the reference to the verse, but even after twenty years of ministry he could not remember where in the Bible it was found.

"So, what do we do when God does not act like we think He should?" asked Hank.

Tom was quiet, as he was mentally trying to locate God under an enormous pile of shoulds.

"Tom?" asked Hank.

"God owes me," said Tom. "Is this the epitome of shoulding on God? We try our best to follow God's plan for our lives, so we feel He owes us in return."

Hank was quiet for a long moment. Tom knew what he was waiting for. He took a deep breath, and said:

"*I* believe that God owes me," said Tom.

"I believe the reason I should on God so easily and so often is that I believe He owes me."

"Explain," Hank prompted gently, "what does God owe you?"

Tom took another deep breath. This was hard to say. But maybe if he said it out loud, to someone else, it wouldn't come bursting out of him from the inside when he was alone anymore.

"He owes me my dad back, for starters. My dad left his job and our family and gave his life to serving others. God took him before any of us could even say goodbye.

"He also owes me financial margin to do more things with my family. I left my college and career path to pursue His calling. And to be honest, God doesn't pay very well. Truthfully, Hank, I feel like God owes me a raise!

"I see people all over my neighborhood who have left God in the dust, and yet they have one hundred times the financial blessing that I do. My neighbor has a new car every six months, and I'm still driving a 1991 Accord and praying that April's 2001 Saturn, that they don't even make anymore, keeps orbiting our city and getting her from place to place.

"I know that finance isn't really a blessing, and the Bible says the meek shall inherit the earth. But couldn't I inherit a little something right now?!

"Frankly, it's embarrassing to pull into the church parking lot on a Sunday morning and have the oldest car in the community. Even though I know God's love is more important than money, does everybody else remember that, too? Or do they just think I'm a bad provider?"

Even as he said this, Tom heard himself and winced.

"There you go," Hank reminded him. "Getting mixed up about your audience again."

"Right." Tom took a deep breath. "Other people are not the authority in my life. God is. And I'll bet I can guess which He prefers, between me driving a sports car and me being a leader who lives to serve others."

But Tom wasn't done quite yet. After a moment of silence, he said:

"There's one more thing; God owes me happiness."

As soon as he said it, he felt wrong, but the words felt right.

"I have given up so much for the church," the words exploded out of him. "I labor over messages more than even God knows! I meet with people I don't know and neglect those I know and love. I have allowed my family to live in a glass house that everyone feels free to cast stones toward, so we can set a good example.

"And I just often feel like God has not kept up His end of the bargain! So often, I don't feel very happy."

"His end of the bargain," Hank said softly.

"Yes," Tom said firmly. "His end of the bargain. I have done all of this for Him. I should be happy, right?"

"I think you just should on yourself," said Hank. Then he paused for a moment. "Without sounding uncaring, Tom, God does not owe you anything. All of these private pacts and contracts you've made with God in your head over the years have been one-sided.

"It's not as though you sat down with God and said, 'I'll be your pastor, but only if you promise me money and happiness out of the deal. And only if you give me my dad back.' If you had tried that, Tom, what do you think would have happened?"

"God would have said, 'Nope, not gonna happen,'" Tom admitted. "He would have told me that if I wanted money, I should do something else."

"And what about the rest?" Hank prompted gently.

"He would have told me that I'd see my dad again in Heaven, but I couldn't turn back time. He would have told me that nobody is happy all the time, not even pastors."

"And what would you have done?" Hank asked.

Tom thought back to that summer internship at his dad's little country church and how good it felt to help all of those people. He knew the answer instantly. "I would have become a pastor anyway!" he said.

"Right," Hank agreed. "So your dad, money, happiness - that was never part of the deal. And you've known that, at some level, from the beginning.

"It's not that God doesn't love you or want to bless you in all the ways you have mentioned. But God is not bound to our contracts. And sometimes what we think is good for us really isn't. Would you be happier if you had more money, but no team or community to lead?"

"Probably not," Tom admitted.

"As I mentioned to you earlier, God rarely acts like we think He should. And just like with other people, we often expect things of Him even though we know they're not reasonable. It's a sobering day when we realize that we have spent years shoulding on God.

"This is not a spiritual statement," Hank explained. "It's not just about religious life. This is something that all humans do. We make one-sided contracts and bargains with God, often without actually running them by Him first. And then when God doesn't live up to His end of the deal, we should on Him. And this leads us down one of two different paths."

"Either we choose to continue to trust God, even though He frankly seems untrustworthy based on His failure to deliver on the bargains He never agreed to. Or we choose to blame Him and decide not to pray to Him anymore.

"Here is what I want you to know: God not acting like He should is nothing new. Since the dawn of creation, God has been doing His own thing, in His own time, in His own way!

"Consider Joseph from the book of Genesis.

"Joseph is a guy who had every right to should on God. So many unfair things happened to him. But he did not blame God for those things. He chose to trust God even when God did not act like Joseph probably thought He should. And that allowed Joseph to move from a should life to a very good life. All of his misfortunes ended up placing him in one of the most powerful positions in the land.

"Is your Bible on your desk, Tom?" Hank asked, though he must have known the answer.

"Let's start in Genesis, Chapter 37," Hank suggested, "and consider all of the shoulds that could have entered into Joseph's mind.

"He could have should on his family as his own brothers beat him, threw him in a pit and sold him into slavery.

"He could have should on his boss as he was falsely accused of something he did not do, treated unfairly and thrown into prison.

"He could have should on his friends in prison, who when released from prison forgot about him for two years and left him alone in his cell.

"And what about the king? He could have should on the king who just wanted to use Joseph for his own benefit when he couldn't understand God.

"Joseph was misunderstood and mistreated by his family, his friends, his employer, and the ruler of the land.

"He could have should on God.

"Maybe he should have should on God!

"I have personally should on God for far less.

"But Joseph decided to trust God rather than should on Him, and that is the key to getting past this specific faith-destroying should: Trust God even when you are not sure that you should."

As Hank spoke, Tom sensed that his course in shoulds was coming to an end.

But could he really let go of all of these shoulds?

Tom remembered how he had felt that first week after talking to Hank.

There's your incentive, he thought to himself. *Freedom.*

Chapter 28

"God's plan for your life preceded your plan for your life," Hank began. "God knows exactly what you are supposed to do."

Tom was surprised to find the words liberating. That could be seen as a way of saying, 'no' to Tom's own plans for his life. But instead, it felt like reassurance that he was on the right path, whether he thought so or not.

> *"For we are God's workmanship, created in*
> *Christ Jesus to do good works, which God prepared*
> *in advance for us to do". - Ephesians 2:10*

"God had plans for your life before you had plans for your life.

"The reason we must trust is because He sees things we don't see as He leads us toward His good plans. When God doesn't act like we think He should, there is a reason! We just can't see the whole picture.

> *"My thoughts are nothing like your thoughts,"*
> *says the LORD. "And my ways are far beyond*
> *anything you could imagine." - Isaiah 55:8*

"Oh yeah. Isaiah 55," Tom filed away the reference, embarrassed that he hadn't known it off the top of his head.

"Tom, I know this is not easy, but you must choose to trust God even when He doesn't act like you think He should. Because He created you on purpose, and He has a plan for your life. If you choose not to trust the plan, well, the plan won't change."

Tom was quiet.

"This is wrecking me, you know," he said finally. "I have spent so many years, especially recently, shoulding on God as I told myself I was serving Him. Realizing what a hypocrite I've been is overwhelming.

"I feel like a fraud.

"I feel like I tell everyone to trust God.

"Then I don't trust Him myself.

"I tell everyone not to judge others.

"Then I judge them myself.

"I tell others 'only God can judge you.' Then I assume God's position and judge them myself."

Hank gave a moment of respectful silence once Tom was finished speaking. Finally, he said, "Listen, Tom, God has a perfect track record of faithfulness. He is not going to blow it by abandoning you!

"Luckily for us, God is not bound to abide by human desires. Can you imagine what a mess the world would be if He did everything that everyone thought He should?

"But He is bound to love you.

"He is bound to never leave you.

"He is bound by His own nature to be faithful to you, even when you are not faithful to Him.

"I once heard a pastor say: 'Our faith is not in our own faith, but in the faithfulness of our God.'

"That has to be true of you, Tom. Just because you are a man of faith does not mean you perfectly understand or exhibit faith. No human is perfect. That's the whole reason Jesus came.

"The Bible is full of people of faith who should on God. Because, again, God hardly ever acts like we think He should. Some great prophets trusted and accepted God's will; others most definitely did not. He loved them and guided them, just the same.

Hank paused again. "What will you do with this newfound awareness, Tom? How will you move yourself and others from a should life to a good life?"

Tom was silent.

"Think about that," Hank said, "and let's talk again when you are ready."

Tom heard the soft click as Hank hung up, leaving Tom alone with his thoughts and feelings.

Wow, that was like a mic drop, thought Tom. *A very gentle, loving mic drop.*

Tom felt like part of himself had died that day on the phone. A part of his self-image as a perfectly faithful servant had been recalibrated and chipped away.

There was so much he needed to thank Hank for, but he decided it could wait until he had answers to Hank's questions.

Now that Tom had been gifted with more self awareness he knew that his old self-image must be released; he had to find something to replace it with.

Could he do it? Tom wondered.

What would his new image and identity be?

Grace, said a small voice in Tom's mind. *Not duty, but grace.*

Tom promised to do his best to make that true.

He promised to meet up with grace more often in his daily life.

Chapter 29

The mug was stained, and the brown leather chair was creased, comfortable and old. Tom was up early on Tuesday morning looking out of the window in his small study at home. The falling snow looked blue as the sun began to peek through the predawn clouds.

It was the week before Christmas. What a month it had been. Tom felt in some ways as though Christmas had come early for him, as Hank had given him the gift of four weekly phone calls. The calls had given Tom a key he needed to unlock a door that had seemed sealed forever, a door to a happy past, where Christmas was his favorite season, the door to a good life.

Tom felt different.

He felt free.

He wanted those he led and loved to experience this same freedom. He knew so many of them struggled with never-ending lists of shoulds, frustrations with other people, and even frustrations with God. In their rush to do what they thought they should, they exhausted themselves, and then should all over everyone else.

Tom looked at his calendar for the new year. There were all kinds of appointments that he was sure he would keep, but there was also a January sermon series about Jonah he had put on the calendar six months ago. And that, that could be amended.

He had to help the members of his church meet their shoulds.

He had to help free them from themselves.

The next four hours felt like four minutes as Tom's fingers flew over his keyboard. His conversations with Hank, and the stark realizations they triggered, poured out from his fingers.

I should on God when…
I should on others when…
Others should on me when…

The message outlines and content came easily. Tom felt young again. Words hadn't flowed so easily since he was a new preacher, when everything about the role seemed exciting and new.

He no longer dreamed of leaving his work and church.

Now he was excited to be part of it.

It was amazing how God, through a trusted friend, could fix in one month what Tom could not have accomplished on his own in ten years!

The week leading up to Christmas was light. Tom felt almost like a child whose parent had him on their shoulders. It was as if nothing could threaten or touch Tom because of his position, safe in the knowledge of who he was.

Leading a church of thousands meant many parties and get-togethers with new and old friends around Christmas. In the past Tom had accepted about half of the invitations, letting April attend the rest alone making half-true excuses for Tom's absence.

But this year was different. Tom's recent realizations had granted him a new-found freedom and energy. Tom felt alive, and he again loved the week before Christmas. And the parties were no longer an intrusion into his calling. They were a gift.

This was again his favorite time of the year.

***

By late afternoon the day before Christmas Eve, Tom was effortlessly finishing the Christmas Eve message.

As he typed the final punctuation to end the last message of the year, he realized what the first series of the new year must be titled.

He already had four weeks' worth of topics to share.

He began work on a completely new series of January messages, filled with life, energy, and trust in God.

This was not a series borrowed from a big-time church.

It wasn't a re-hashing of anything he'd taught before.

This was as organic, original, fresh, and new as anything in Tom's life had ever been.

Tom closed the computer that evening with messages for the first month of the new year already outlined on his computer. Free of this burden because he trusted in the message that flowed through him, Tom enjoyed Christmas day and the following week without worry or care.

"Tom," April said, looking at him strangely as he laughed over hot cocoa with Thomas, "What did Hank say to you? You act like you're twenty-five again."

Tom turned to April, his eyes sparkling. "I have a new series to share with the congregation, and I wonder if you would be willing to team teach with me one week.

"By the way, April, how's your latest book coming?"

"Writing is hard," said April.

And both of them laughed at how a baby could be born in less than a year, but sometimes a book took almost a decade!

★★★

As they laughed, April felt younger than she'd felt in twenty years.

Tom was finally *seeing* her again. He seemed to have remembered what they'd had together, and what she could do.

"I'd love to team up with you and share the teaching on one of your messages, Tom," she enthused, her eyes sparkling, "on one condition."

Tom raised his eyebrows, taken aback. "What's that?"

"I get your input and teamwork on my book project."

Tom was laughing again. "Deal," he said.

And they shook on it.

Chapter 30

As Tom walked onto the stage on the first Sunday of the new year, he felt like he was stepping into a whole new way of life. A life of grace.

As he faced his rapt congregation, the words projected onto the screen behind him read:

"Should Happens"

"Welcome to a new year and a new series," Tom enthused. "This year, we're going to talk about something that you may have never thought about before. It's helping to make me into a new man, and I promise, it will help you, too."

Whispers went up across the auditorium, excited at the prospect of something fresh and new.

"This should be good," Tom heard one woman whisper.

To download free digital copies of all four message outlines of Tom's "Should Happens" series go *toddclark.org*

THE WEDDING

I hope you enjoyed your opportunity to Meet The Shoulds. There is just one part of their story missing, and it's a very important part: Tom and April's wedding.

I worked for months on many versions of their wedding, with so many possibilities in mind. Would everything be blissfully perfect, like their gifts for each other, or their holiday together?

Or would they face unprecedented challenges, and find themselves with opportunities to rest in grace despite things not going as they should?

Which do you think better captures Tom and April's life together? I am not the one to write of the heavenly or hellacious day.

Would you write this chapter of their lives?

Go to:

toddclark.com

You'll see a tab called **"SHOULD HAPPENS"**

Take some time to write and read all the versions of Tom and April's big day.

Which ones go the way they should?

Which ones don't - and as a consequence, offer opportunities for grace?

THE SHOULDS

I should on myself.
I convene courtrooms in my mind.

I should on others.
I have secret job descriptions for everyone I meet.

Others should on me.
People expect their personal "to do list" to be carried out in my life.

I should on God.
I know how God should act, and then He doesn't.

MEET YOUR SHOULDS

Tom's mentor, Hank, offers him four phone calls to help him identify the shoulds in his life, and change his relationship to them. He asks Tom questions that get right to the heart of the problem, and he asks Tom to examine himself.

Here, we're going to do the same for you.
This six-session guide will help you join Tom on his journey from a should life to a good life.

Session 1

Where Our Shoulds Come From

What kind of town did you grow up in? Was it a lot like Green Springs, or very different?

_____

What values and value judgements did your hometown instill in you? Did people in your hometown prize wealth and hard work, creating both helpful and harmful shoulds in the process? Or did they have a different attitude, with different helpful and harmful-shoulds of their own?

_____

_____

Take some time to write out, privately reflect, and share with your group some details of your early years.

_____

_____

_____

_____

What is your favorite time of the year, and why?

_____

This past year, did you really embrace and enjoy that "favorite"

season? _____

_____

When is the first time you can remember feeling like you should do

something? _____

_____

What's one thing the people back home would say you should do
that's good, such as working hard or helping your neighbor?

_____

What's one thing the people back home would say you should do
that might not always lead to something good?

_____

Can you relate to the "courtroom of the mind" that Tom subjects
himself to where he is prosecutor, judge and jury? Think about a
time when you quietly convened a courtroom in your mind:

_____

_____

I convene mental courtrooms: (check one)

Hourly ☐   Daily   ☐   Weekly ☐

Tom's family has a lot to do with his story and journey. How did

you grow up? _____

_____

Did your parents live in the shoulds? _____

How did they transfer these pressures to you? _____

_____

When did you feel like you were "doing good," growing up?

_____

_____

When did you feel like you had failed to meet your family's expectations?

_____

_____

Were these influences always good? Or did they sometimes lead to running on empty, or getting your priorities out of order?

_____

At times, Tom felt his father was giving his best to those he knew the least. Did you ever feel like that growing up? Do you ever do that today with friends or family?

_____

_____

What were you passionate about growing up? _____

_____

What passions from your early years are still part of your life today?

_____

_____

Do you ever wish you had more time to spend with people who are important to you? _____

_____

Why don't you have that time? What gets in the way?

_____

What would you do with that time, if you had it?_____

_____

_____

If I woke up tomorrow and my life was perfect, it would mean I

had started: _____

_____ and stopped _____

_____.

Do you have a mentor, like Hank, in your life? _____

Is there someone in your life who you really admire, want to be
like, or could learn a lot from?

_____

Could you ask them for advice from time to time?

_____

What questions would you ask them, if you could? (List at least 3.)

_____

_____

_____

Which questions *will* you ask them this week? (Choose one.)

_____

Session 2

I Should On Myself When...

Hank asks Tom: "Who do you hope will applaud you?" In your life, how would you answer that question?

_____

Do you ever feel like you are competing in "an unwinnable race?" How does that make you feel on the inside?

_____

When I take a break from work, I feel: _____

_____

_____

_____.

What do you think of the statement: "Not everything that is true is noble?" _____

What do you think of the statement: "The Devil thrives on our fear?"

_____

What do you think of the statement: "God is love?"

_____

What are some "good shoulds" in your life? (List at least 7.)

_____

_____

_____

_____

_____

_____

_____

If you had to choose just three "big rock" shoulds out of that list, which three fill you with the most love?

_____   _____   _____

Write about a time when you should on yourself: _____

_____

_____

_____

When you do not have the time or energy to care about the things that you know you should care about…what do you usually do?

_____

How do you feel about the idea of "stewarding your compassion?" What does that mean to you?

_____

_____

What are some ways you could steward your compassion each week, so that you have care to give to those you truly care about?

_____

Do you ever compare yourself to other people you see in public or on social media? What is the result of that comparison?

_____

Do you think those comparisons are accurate? Or do you think the people you compare yourself to actually have problems very much like your own?

_____

Do you find it harder to extend grace to yourself or to others? Why?

_____

How do you relate to Tom's thoughts where he says: "I see every opportunity as an obligation. I see every invitation as an investigation or commentary on my commitment of whether or not I care enough about a person or cause?"

_____

Create your own start-doing and stop-doing lists.

This week I will start...

_____

This week I will stop...

_____

Do you have a "thin space" place in your life?

_____

When I am _____

_____ the distance between me and God seems to shrink.

Session 3

I Should On Others When...

What was your first job? _____

How does your first job overlap or share similarities with the job you have today? _____

What is the worst job you have ever had? What made it so uncomfortable? _____

_____

What is the best job you've ever had, and what did you love about it?

_____

What do you dislike about your job today?

_____

What's your favorite part of your job today?

_____

Have you ever had a job without a job description? How did that go?

_____

Can you relate to having "secret job descriptions" for people in your life? What people in your life might you be placing these private burdens on? _____

_____

When people don't meet your expectations ... how do you feel about them? _____

Do you ever put "price tags" on people you meet? If so, would you say you typically value others higher or lower than yourself?

_____

_____

Hank says to Tom, "The shoulds are like a boomerang. The more you should on others, the more they will should on you." How have you experienced this in your life?

_____

_____

_____

Session 4

Others Should On Me When...

Recall a time in your life when you were in a car that literally ran out of gas. Why did that happen? _____

_____

Where is the needle on your personal fuel tank today? (Check one.)

Full ☐   Half Full   ☐   Empty ☐

Can you relate to this sentence? "When Tom was empty, sin was close."

_____

I feel most susceptible to sin when _____

_____

_____

_____

Who in your life do you feel like has tried or is currently trying to run your life? _____

Has anyone ever made you feel like you'd be a bad person if you said 'no' to them? _____

Why is it hard to say 'no' to others' input, ideas and invitations?

_____

_____

Jesus was the greatest servant to ever walk this planet – yet He still said 'no' often. When have you said 'no' to...

• A friend? _____

_____

• Peer pressure and/or promotions? _____

• Helping a good person with a solvable problem?

_____

What are the pros and cons of stewarding your compassion?

_____

When I am obsessed with saying yes to others, I feel like my life

is: _____

_____.

When I am obsessed with saying yes to God, I feel like my life is:

_____

_____.

Hank talks about how important it is "to go up on the mountain and be filled by God." How does this notion make you feel?

_____

Where is your "mountain" that you can retreat to for God to fill you up?

_____

_____

Session 5

I Should on God When...

Think about a time when God did not act like you thought He should. _____

_____

When God didn't act like I thought He should, I immediately

_____

_____

When God didn't act like I thought He should, I eventually

_____

_____

_____

List some of the private pacts and contracts you have had with God:

• If I _____, then God should
_____.

• If I _____, then God should
_____.

• If I _____, then God should
_____.

• If I _____, then God should
_____.

• If I _____, then God should
_____.

• If I _____, then God should
_____.

What do you believe God owes you? _____

Put a check mark next to where you currently stand with God.

Trust ☐   Confused   ☐   Blame ☐

Ephesians 2:10 - *"For we are God's workmanship, created in Christ Jesus to do good works, which God prepared in advance for us to do."*

How do you feel about the idea that God's plan for your life preceded your own plans for your life, and the plans that other people have for your life? _____

_____

Do you believe that God has a perfect track record of faithfulness, and He is not going to blow it by abandoning you?

_____

How would your week be different, if you lived in that truth?

_____

Session 6

Now we've covered the four most important types of shoulds. Let's cement this teaching by creating some practical steps we can carry out in our daily lives moving forward from a should life to a good life.

Rank the shoulds below in order from 1 to 4, with 1 being "the should I struggle with the most" and 4 being "the should that is easiest for me to let go of."

I wrestle with the shoulds in this order:

_____ I should on myself
_____ I should on others
_____ Others should on me
_____ I should on God

In order to move from a should life to a good life I need to do these things things …

I need to stop trying to… _____

_____

 I need to start stewarding my compassion, filling myself up and refreshing myself by…_____

_____

Since meeting The Shoulds, I plan to..._____

_____

I need to share this book and the concept of The Shoulds with

_____

Join us online

On the ***toddclark.org*** website there is a tab for SHOULD HAPPENS. This destination contains the latest stories and happenings with the book, as well as a speaking calendar for Todd's speaking engagements.

Toddclark.org

@toddclark - Twitter

@todd_clark - Instagram

Facebook.com/toddclark

About the Author

Todd Clark is a creative, innovative, team-focused, results-driven leader with a unique blend of life experience. Todd is the Vice President of Senior Leadership at Slingshot Group, a coaching and staffing firm. Todd has 28 years of leadership experience in nonprofit organizations sized between 200 and 24,000. Todd speaks often around the nation and monthly at Parkview Christian Church that has multiple campuses around Chicagoland. Todd is the founder of "Eat Art" - a nonprofit photography organization committed to artfully ending hunger. Todd enjoys golf, coffee with friends, VW buses and surf photography. Todd is married to his high school sweetheart, René, and they have two amazing children, Ruby and Cole, and a true gift in a son-in-law, Cole Kedney. Todd and René live in Huntington Beach, California.